CARIBBEAN

HUSTLE

DOUGLAS BEATTY

ISBN 978-1-7324567-3-0
Library of Congress Control Number: 2019935738

Published by Legal Eagle Beagle & Briefcase
Rancho Mirage, CA
doug@douglasbeatty.com

Visit amazon.com to order additional copies.

The first Craps game is mentioned in Greek mythology.

Zeus, Poseidon, and Hades played for shares of the Universe.

Poseidon won the Oceans.

Hades won the Underworld.

Zeus won the Heavens but was suspected of having used loaded dice.

Preface

Much of what occurs in this book actually happened as described, and many of the characters are based on people I've known. The country of Balboa is a composite of places where I lived or visited during one or more of my previous lives.

Many of the events are inspired by personal experiences, however self-preservation has dictated that some freedoms be taken when describing certain exploits and people. And readers may think that Balboa bears a striking resemblance to the Commonwealth of the Bahamas. But of course that would only be speculation.

Some names have been changed because not everyone included would be thrilled to see his or her real name in print. And because I want to be around to perhaps, write another book, I've found it prudent to exercise some discretion. Case in point is the hit man. Back in the day, I knew this guy very well. He even sponsored a Little League baseball team for me when I was stuck for league financial support. However, it wasn't until more than twenty-five years later that I learned what his true profession had been during the time we were hanging out together. And the bank robber wannabe? Again, I knew him well. He often ate at our home, came to our parties, and coached in the YMCA youth baseball league that I started in Freeport, Bahamas. And while it's hard to believe, Ozzie actually did knock himself out in the parking lot of a bank while trying to pretend he had just been robbed.

Former Canadian heavyweight boxing champion George Chuvalo is included because he has always been one of my heroes. I regretted not having him appear in my previous book, *It's Always a Game*, but I didn't want to impose on him at the time. George used to date my first wife's roommate, so I knew him during that rodeo. Also, when I returned to Toronto after working as a Craps dealer at the Fremont Hotel in Las Vegas, I played cards and booked bets at various used car lots along Bloor Street West in Toronto. George was a frequent and formidable player during that time. But I can no longer resist. He is such an enduring Canadian icon, and he has made such a huge contribution by speaking out against drug and alcohol abuse, that I'm thinking what the hell, if this book attracts a lot of attention, or if the television pilot based on It's Always a Game gets any traction, maybe he'll benefit from the publicity.

I've also included, with considerable trepidation, the KFC story and the tale about Marco and the Wave Runner. Actually, I put them in and took them out several times but finally decided that the stories are too good not to be included. As such, I've at least partially (or perhaps temporarily) overcome my fear. Reading on, you'll understand the reasons for my concern. Again, these events actually happened. And although it has been quite a while, I don't want to include the real names of those involved: I'm pretty sure they'd be more than just a little cranky.

So between you and me, I've decided to gamble a little, put them in, and hope they're all dead.

The bottom line is that writing this book has rekindled many memories and has allowed me to revisit many episodes from my past. It's been a trip. And if I have offended anyone along the way, may I offer my apologies now. In particular, if I've offended Sy or Ozzie or Marco, I hope that we can let bygones remain bygones. All of us only have enough time left to play "just once more around the table," and who needs more aggravation?

Finally, my thanks to those who knew that I was writing another book, and who have graciously let me tell their stories, regardless.

Douglas Beatty

Prologue

I started out pitching pennies, playing cards, and shooting dice. Poker, Craps, proposition bets, sports pools—it all came easy to me. I even started selling Christmas trees in my early teens: I could always find a way to hustle a buck. Eventually I ran a barely legal, charity-blessed card room and an Internet gaming site. They were hugely successful. I made a ton of money, and everyone called me an entrepreneur. And then I lost a ton of money and everyone thought I had been crazy to have risked it all. But what did they know? Looking back, I realize I'm just a guy who gambles. It's what I am. It's all I am.

Chance Daly

Chapter One

I'd rather be lucky than good,
but if I had my choice,
just give me timing
—The pool players, gamblers, and bookmakers
Plantation Bowling Alley, Toronto, Canada

Beautiful, blond, wife Debbie and I made our way onto the crowded Air Balboa aircraft and found our seats about midway back. It was a smaller jet—not a puddle jumper exactly, but not a flying palace like the A380 Airbus, either.

I had flown on the A380 precisely once. I had splurged on a first class ticket back in the day when I was on a roll. But now, as Debbie and I took our slightly cramped seats, it was a reminder of how much our status in life had ratcheted downward. But I also knew that this trip had the potential to change all that.

However I was so wrapped up in reflection and self-pity that I hadn't noticed how quiet Debbie was. Usually she was a happy traveler, chatty and at ease. But if I had been paying closer attention, I would have noticed that her face was pale, and her lips were pressed into a thin line as she stared toward the front of the plane with what I now know was dread. But I was too wrapped up in myself at the moment to think about what she might be going through.

But if Debbie and I weren't having the best day of our lives, Norm, aka Catcher, seated a couple of rows behind us, was living it up. Norm was my former second-in-command at our Churches in Action (CIA) charity-blessed card room. He isn't my partner, exactly, but he is far more than just my right-hand man. The name *Catcher* fits perfectly and epitomizes exactly what you think of as a baseball catcher: medium height, squat, and thick all over. But his brain doesn't fit the jock profile. He's as sharp as they come. He also has that *can do* mentality, and the tougher the job, the more apt I am to give it to Catcher. And I know that if war ever breaks out, I'd definitely want to be on his side. He's going to be essential to me in this new venture. And I owe him. He has been with me through thick and thin and stuck around when things were a whole lot worse than they are now.

When I was a kid, I began gambling by tossing pennies and sports cards closest to the wall, and betting on about any game I could find. Within a couple of years after leaving high school, and with thanks to Father Anthony and his parish, I started a barely legal, charity-blessed card room and mini casino. With his help, we obtained a license for a Catholic charity. This license allowed us, for a Christian share of the profits, to operate a poker room and bingo parlor. I knew a lot about gambling when we opened, but over the years, I got my PhD from the School of Hard Knocks. And it was that experience that really helped me hit one out of the park. After a few years in business, I could see how the industry was evolving, and I became an early entrant into Internet gaming. We were incredibly successful. I made a ton of money. But did I take my chips off the table? No. I'm too smart for that. I kept "rollin' dem bones." I took the ten million dollars I received from the sale of my Internet gaming site, Gambleraction.com, and figured I was on my way to making a hundred million. That was my goal. *A hundred million.* Wow, the things I could do with that kind of bread! I even toyed with the idea of buying the Toronto Argos football team or bringing an NFL team to southern Ontario.

But how do I get from the minors to the big leagues? How does a guy parlay a small fortune into a large fortune? I sought advice, talked to a lot of people, and finally decided the biggest Craps game in the world was going to be my arena: The Stock Market. Wall Street. Bay Street. Fortunes are made there every day. It seemed like the perfect fit.

And for once in my life, I went the cautious route. I thought I'd ease in. I started by buying small amounts of blue chip stocks. And what could be more solid than the banks? So I bought Bank of America at forty-five dollars. BAC went to fifty in no time. I bought Citibank at forty-five, and it quickly climbed to fifty-four. I was making money hand over fist.

But even I knew that stock markets don't go straight up forever—there are the inevitable corrections. I wasn't worried by these. I saw them as buying opportunities. When my stocks ramped up I'd sell a bunch, and when my stocks backed off a bit, I'd step back in and buy more. It worked perfectly—until 2007 when the crash hit.

Of course, I didn't see it as a crash. To me, it just looked like a temporary downturn, the perfect opportunity to double down. It was simple. Whenever the market went down a couple of hundred points in a day, I thought of it as a wonderful chance to reload. I mean, markets always go back up. Right?

So when BAC went from $55 to $40, I bought more. And when Citibank went from $50 to $25, I bought more. Then BAC went to $30 and then $20, then $10, and I kept on buying. It finally bottomed out at about $3.50. Citibank eventually went as low as $0.90. I kept buying until I couldn't buy anymore.

Then the margin calls began. I soon learned that brokerage houses have no sense of humor and even less patience. Forced to sell at the lowest point in the market crash, most of my $10 million became dust in the rearview mirror.

But the good news is that I learned something important about myself. I learned that I'm just a guy who gambles. It's what I am. It's all I am. And, although it took some time, I finally realized that I could make this setback temporary. All I needed was a new game and fresh action. As my dad would say, "Quit your whining. Deal the cards."

I was wrenched back to the present when the plane shook suddenly then dropped like a falling elevator. For a second everyone was too shocked to react—we were just trying to catch our breath. But then screams drowned out the whine of the jet engines as we fell through the sky.

Debbie gripped my arm, her fingernails digging deep into my flesh. And then she did something I'd never known her to do. She shrieked at the top of her lungs: repeatedly, loudly. She was in a full-blown panic, and all I could do was hold her close. I thought I may never get another chance to speak to her again and leaned close to her ear and said, "I love you, Debbie. I love you so much." I'm not sure she even heard me.

Then as suddenly as it had started, it was over. We didn't crash into the sea. The plane righted itself and once again we were moving smoothly through the air. The entire episode had probably taken less than ten seconds, if that. But they were the longest ten seconds of my life.

The intercom crackled, and we heard the voice of the pilot. "Sorry about that," he said, in an evenly modulated tone. Do they teach all pilots to use that voice? Is that a course in flight school? "That was a little more than we bargained for," he said.

"Those of you who frequently fly to the Caribbean know that it's pretty common to experience dry-air turbulence when we cross the shoreline and head out to sea. But that was a lot rougher than usual. It was so unexpected I spilled my coffee. You should see the front of my pants."

"Yeah, and you should see the *back* of mine!" yelled Norm. His wisecrack got a bigger laugh than it deserved—everyone was so happy to be alive that we roared as if he were a Vegas comedian. From the time we boarded, Norm had been trying to flirt with a cute flight attendant but had been getting nowhere. However his well-timed punch line relieved a lot of the angst and fear of the passengers, and as such, he had made her job a lot easier. So for the rest of the flight, she made sure Norm was well taken care of. He always had a drink in one hand and a snack in the other, and before we landed, he had her phone number and plans for dinner once he was back in Toronto.

But while Norm was doing his best George Clooney impersonation, I had to untangle myself from Debbie's death grip. She was babbling away about how sorry she was that she had screamed. I pulled up the armrest between us and held her close and said, "Don't worry, Deb. It's OK now."

I was worried about her. Debbie was always totally cool and in control. Nothing fazed my wife. She had a self-confident aura that commanded attention and respect. Panic was totally out of character.

"I know it's crazy," she said, "but recently I've been having nightmares about dying in a plane crash. There's a bang, a shudder, and the plane spirals down. Thank God I wake up just before it hits the ground. Each time I'm bathed in sweat just like now. It's awful to feel so stupid. I haven't said anything, but it's scary how similar it is to what just happened."

Chapter Two

Do we choose our destiny or does our destiny choose us?
—Chance Daly, Grand Balboa

With palm trees, blue skies, and eighty-degree temperatures to greet us, how bad could this trip be? It had been five below zero and snowing when Debbie, Norm, and I flew out of Toronto International, and a trip to the Caribbean country of Balboa had sounded pretty damn good. Balboa is a small country made up of three large islands only seventy-five miles apart and located less than one hundred miles off the coast of Florida. The population is predominately black and whose forefathers were brought to the islands as slaves to mine salt. Other than the sea, sun, and sand, the islands have few natural features and no industry other than tourism. As a result, government agencies are the most significant source of employment other than tourist-related facilities, including hotels, bars, and restaurants.

One quickly learns that the notion that all Caribbean countries are populated by thousands of swaying palm trees is totally inaccurate. Balboa is nothing like Jamaica or Cuba. Those islands have mountains, cliffs, waterfalls, and multicolored flora, creating breathtaking vistas. Balboa's islands are flat sandbars by comparison, with the fifty-mile-long boomerang-shaped Grand Balboa being the only one with any elevation at all. Grand Balboa has a thirty-foot-high ridge that travels ten miles right down the middle. The rest of the land is low, flat, and covered by scrub pine trees. But the Balboa islands do enjoy beautiful warm tropical sunshine and offer soft pink sand beaches and the bluest waters in the Atlantic. And Grand Balboa now has palm trees—each one imported by hotel and resort developers. And that thirty-foot-high ridge? *When de winds blow, and the surge from de hurricane come, it's the only place to be.*

Having lost almost all the money that I had received from the sale of my Internet gaming site, it took a while for me to pick myself up off the canvas. However, after a few months of stepping on my lip, I shook it off, felt a little more energized, and bit by bit I became a little more focused on scoping out a new venture.

I was even thinking about approaching Father Anthony to see if his Catholic parish would be interested in sponsoring a second casino and bingo operation, but the fates intervened. Out of the blue, I received an invitation from Paul Bethel, the Balboa Deputy Minister of Tourism, to investigate the opportunity of acquiring the King's Own Golf Resort and Casino in the spectacular Caribbean beach town of San Vida.

While he was in Toronto obtaining his MBA, Paul had been a frequent poker player at our Churches in Action operation, better known as the CIA Club. When he returned to Balboa, he made his way rapidly through the ranks, becoming a senior government official. Realizing that what was good for the city of San Vida was also good for his minister, the honorable Charles Symonette, Paul pitched the idea of approaching me to see if I had any interest in taking over the resort. He quickly received the minister's blessing.

The King's Own had been one of the Caribbean's most spectacular golf and casino resorts before it was decimated by the one-two punch of hurricanes, Frances and Jean, in 2004. The resort was one of many hospitality-related properties owned by Diamond Resorts International, a company traded on the New York Stock Exchange. While Diamond Resorts was readying itself to bring this asset back into serviceable condition, its representatives had entered into a series of negotiations with representatives from the Hotel Workers' Union regarding old labor issues. The owners had never been satisfied with the level of service the resort had provided to its guests and was seeking cooperation from the union to help establish better and more effective training programs.

To demonstrate how serious Diamond Resorts was about helping the staff upgrade their skills, it asked the Union to agree that management could terminate any employee who chose not to attend hotel training courses. This was rejected by the Union. When the matter could not be resolved, the labor minister stepped in. At that point, the hotel owners upped the stakes by also asking to be allowed to hire one trained expatriate for every four Balboans.

As tensions escalated, the hotel owners began to harden their position by intimating that they would not reopen the hotel without these concessions. The government and the union then retaliated by taking the issue public with union meetings and inflammatory media interviews. Eventually, Diamond Resorts' senior executives from New York travelled to the capital city of Playas, to meet with both the Minister of Labor and the union leaders. Their goal was to tone down the public rhetoric while explaining the gravity of the situation. They were there to deliver the clear message that the company was not prepared to reopen the hotel until these common-sense concessions were granted.

On the flip side, the government and the union were banking on their thinking that the hotel, casino, and golf courses would fall into ruin if they were left unmaintained and therefore the owners would be forced to do what was necessary to protect their assets. Union representatives began to recite the mantra that "Big business must listen to the people. Big business must cooperate. If they don't, then they must leave. In our land, our people must be first." To add fuel to the fire, labor-union representatives began to repeat their belief that the owners of the hotel had too large an investment to have it lay dormant.

But what they didn't know was that the hotel owners had been growing increasingly concerned with the negative press that was beginning to seep out onto the world media stage. The *Wall Street Journal* had run an article about "Labor Strife in Balboa," and CNN and Fox News had sent journalists with camera crews to San Vida. It wasn't just luck that their arrival happened to coincide with a labor union town hall meeting. It was great fodder for guerrilla journalism. "WE HAVE THEM WHERE WE WANT THEM" screamed one headline.

The headline issue in Balboa was eventually raised at a Diamond Resorts Board of Directors meeting. The chairman had asked the previous general manager of the hotel to attend in case board members had more questions. The GM was succinct and to the point. He stated that with the current labor unrest, he was concerned that even after the hotel was rebuilt, he anticipated ongoing challenges dealing with the increasingly militant labor pool. In exasperation, one board member posed the unthinkable question: "What the hell are we doing there if they don't want us? And if they don't want us, what's our exit strategy?"

Chief Financial Officer Bill Goldberg had recently shared with the chairman that he was in the final negotiations with the insurance company regarding their hurricane insurance claim settlement. A board member then asked if there was any way the company could take the insurance settlement money and not spend it on a re-build or repair of the property. This question had also crossed Goldberg's mind, and with the blessing of the chairman, he had already run the idea by their legal team. The lawyers had quickly confirmed that there was no reason why the owners couldn't simply take the money and allow the property to lie fallow or, more aptly, just sit there baking in the hot Balboan sun.

This idea quickly caught on. One board member said, "This sounds like a hooker deal. We've got it. We're going to get money for it. And we'll still have it." After the laughter subsided, the board unanimously decided that the hotel's general manager, two of their New York lawyers, and Goldberg, should meet the Balboan minister of labor, Mr. Rolle, and the head of the labor union, Arthur McKenzie, to ensure that the message from the board was fully understood by the union and the government.

The Diamond Resorts' team was instructed to do everything they could to help the other side understand that the hotel owners wanted to be responsible corporate citizens. But they also wanted an assurance that they would have the cooperation of the government and the union to bring about the necessary improvements in both the quality of personnel and the overall attitude of the staff, without which Diamond Resorts would not reopen King's Own.

The meeting did not go well. The union leader had a copy of Diamond Resorts' annual report and became belligerent. He went on and on about how much profit the ownership group was making. "Furthermore," he snarled, "these obscene profits are being made on the backs of our people."

That was about all the hotel team could take. Goldberg said gently, "Mr. McKenzie, please look at how much the King's Own Resort represents on the asset side of the ledger."

When the union representative couldn't find the King's Own as a line item, Mr. Rolle asked to look at the annual report as well. He studied the document for a moment or two and couldn't find it, either. "It's because it's not there," said Goldberg. "But if you look further you'll find a line for other assets. The King's Own is included in that category. Gentlemen, the King's Own is important to all of us in this room. But to our parent company, it is a relatively small investment. And, plainly speaking, our company does not want its name tarnished by association with labor unrest. Furthermore, it does not want ongoing labor problems or to own a property of which it would be less than proud. Please be assured that we recognize the responsibility we have to the thirteen hundred employees of the hotel, casino, and golf courses. Please also know that we want to do everything we can to provide well-paying jobs, and we are willing to invest money in the training of our valuable staff. However, there must be a Balboan quid pro quo. We need a union agreement that allows us to require the staff to attend these training courses as dictated by management. We also need to allow management to make personnel changes as they see fit, without being held hostage every time they need to dismiss an employee. The bottom line is that we want to create and operate a facility in which all stakeholders can take pride. That includes management, staff, owners, and union members, as well as the government. I'm sad to say that previously the service and attitude of personnel at this resort has been poor. As of now, this is completely unacceptable. We need a commitment that all employees will take advantage of our training programs and will embrace the need for change. To accomplish this, we need your assistance."

The union representative and the minister were now backed into a corner. Mr. Rolle protested, "We don't like foreigners coming here and dictating terms to the government."

Big, black, and belligerent, McKenzie stood up, came around the boardroom table, towered over Goldberg, and spat, "You better open de hotel. And now. We mess you up, you don't do dat!"

Not the least bit intimidated, Goldberg realized that he had done everything he could. He had tried to avoid the appearance that he was delivering an ultimatum, but both the minister and the union boss had taken offense at his remarks. Given time, the minister would probably come to understand the situation from Diamond Resorts' perspective. McKenzie, however, now had a head of steam up and was in no mood to consider anyone's opinion but his own. Efforts were made to placate him by trying to help him understand the reality of the situation, but he would only begin another rant. "No way! No way you goin fire my people without my say so."

When Goldberg could finally get himself heard over the ensuing chaos, he said firmly, "Unless we can come to an understanding that these labor concessions are to be granted, the King's Own Resort is going to remain permanently closed."

.

Chapter Three

When a person retires, the competitive fires cool and the need to excel, to dominate, fades. Conversely, when emerging from a self-imposed hiatus, a guy returns to the fray incredibly pumped!
—Seymour Harris, Rancho Mirage, California

So here I am in beautiful Balboa. Me. Chance Daly. A kid from Toronto who suddenly has a legitimate shot at acquiring a hotel and casino in the Caribbean. It's hard to believe.

The day after our arrival, I called Paul Bethel and made an appointment to visit him at his office. But first, Norm and I could hardly wait to check out the property. We drove over to the resort to at least take a preliminary look prior to our meeting. We were pleased, and somewhat relieved to find that it wasn't in nearly as bad shape as we had feared. Although it had been savaged by the two hurricanes, it had been mothballed well, and subsequently safeguarded by the owners.

In the aftermath of the hurricanes, the owners had planned to bring the resort back into service as quickly as possible. It was only when discussions with the government and the union broke down that they began to consider other options. When they received the insurance settlement of $17 million, it was like manna from heaven to Diamond Resorts. They got the cash, wrote off the asset on their balance sheet, and didn't even have to pay a real-estate commission.

After we'd spent a couple of hours at the site, Norm drove us over to Paul's office.

Paul, Norm, and I were all delighted to see each other again, but mindful of the business at hand, we kept the niceties to a minimum. It was showtime.

"So, Paul, if we can pull this all together, how much backing can we expect from your minister of tourism?" I asked as an opening gambit. "What's his name?"

"Charles Symonette" Paul said.

I then asked, "How serious is he about working with us?"

"Chance, Mr. Symonette is absolutely dedicated to seeing that this resort is brought back on stream," Paul said. "The prime minister is, too. This isn't just a passing fancy. Our government made it a campaign promise that it would get the hotel reopened, and the opposition CLP party isn't letting them forget it. The reopening of the King's Own is a high-profile priority that isn't going away."

Paul's perfectly coiffed, gorgeous black, *Beverly Johnson* look-a-like assistant entered, carrying a tray with three glasses of iced tea. We took a few sips, and Paul continued.

"There's another reality as well. The city of San Vida has a population of less than twenty thousand, and the entire island of Grand Balboa has a population of only thirty thousand. To have a potential employer of over thirteen hundred people stalled because of labor issues is almost unconscionable. Even the union bosses are beginning to feel the pressure and to see the light."

Paul got up and walked around the desk, sitting on its edge, closer to my chair.

"Did you know that after the hurricanes, Playas was flat on its back, too?" he asked. "The entire country was in a funk. Then a number of hoteliers went to the government and said that if the unions would be fair and reasonable, and if the government would relax its immigration policies when it came to hiring hotel executives and senior personnel, the hotel industry would be willing to guarantee that a minimum of five thousand new hotel rooms would be built."

"Did it work?"

Paul smiled. "After much deliberation and gnashing of teeth, the government saw the merit. It took an act of parliament, but once those policies were in place, things worked out pretty well. Look at Playas now compared to San Vida. San Vida gets two passenger ships in a week. Playas gets that many every day. What's more, the employees at the Playas hotels are being paid well, especially compared to other Caribbean counterparts. So the foreign owners really did their part. They were willing to pay for performance. They were willing to pay for good staff. And those living in Playas have come to know and appreciate this."

"Can we accomplish the same thing here in San Vida?" I asked.

Paul nodded. "Absolutely. That's our goal. However, having said that, there's a lot of work to be done. San Vida still doesn't have its act together. The union keeps trying to get more blood out of a shrinking stone. The union officers get more strident and their belligerence rubs off on the members. All these factors have had a negative impact on what should be a tourist Mecca. But at least now the government is willing to step up and pressure the union into making the right decisions. So that part of the equation we've got under control.

"Next we have the Port Authority who is the governing body for all businesses in San Vida. They are really supportive. They will do just about anything to get the resort reopened. They're totally onside. And, finally, we have Diamond Resorts, the owner and operators of the resort. They should be supportive

17

of our desire to see the resort resurrected, but they've been worn down by the union. And they've just received a seventeen million dollar insurance settlement, so we believe they will be just as happy to take their money and ride off into the sunset, particularly as we are willing to indemnify them for any prior legacy or ongoing liability. Between us, we're even prepared to pay them some modest amount recognizing the value of the land. But the cold fact is, that the longer the buildings remain vacant, the more they become a magnet for the homeless and squatters, and a target for vandalism. Long-term, vacant properties are a problem just waiting to happen. And the Diamond Resorts' people are smart folks. They realize their exposure. They know that eventually they are going to have to bite the bullet and do something. The timing is perfect for them to cash out and rid themselves of a potential problem at the same time."

"OK," I said. "It all makes sense, but what if they don't want to sell, or don't want to sell at this time? They could string us along for ten years or more."

"Good question" Paul responded. "Our lawyers have told us that in a worst-case scenario, we can rely on the *Eminent Domain* legislation."

"What's that?" intoned Norm.

"That's a law whereby a government may seize a property for reasons of public safety or if the property is needed for the greater good of the country. Our lawyers tell us we're in a good position on both fronts for all the reasons we've just discussed."

"OK," I said. "I agree this may be a great opportunity, but I won't be able to make it happen—in fact, no one will be able to make it happen—unless there's buy-in from all factions. And as the situation stands, there are a lot of moving parts. So here's the deal—I'm willing to front-end up to five hundred thousand dollars in market studies, structural engineering reports, consultant fees, and general due diligence. That should be enough to tell whether or not we have a viable opportunity. But I don't want to spend all this money, time, and energy unless I have a couple of things understood."

"Such as?" Paul asked.

"To begin with, I want a six-month option to buy the property. In addition, I want a one million dollar break fee in the event that somebody in the government gets cute and isn't willing to see the deal through after we've done all the hard, analytical work."

"A million dollars?"

I smiled and said, "There is probably either a notice clause or a right of first refusal clause in the agreement between the Grand Balboa Port Authority and Diamond Resorts. That being the case, I don't want to be the stalking horse. If we are going to do all this work, we want to be compensated in the event Diamond Resorts suddenly becomes recommitted to reopening the property and pushes us aside. The million bucks will go a long way toward paying us for our time and efforts."

Paul sat there on the edge of the desk for a long moment, thinking over what I had said. Finally he nodded and said, "Well, Chance, I haven't heard anything unreasonable from you. Let's develop a laundry list of matters that have to be addressed. I'll take it to my minister. He'll take it up the ladder to the prime minister, and I think we can cobble together a deal. And, Chance…"

"Yes?"

"No guns."

"What do you mean 'no guns'?" I said.

"No guns means no guns," he said. "In Balboa, even the police don't carry firearms. If, for instance, you forgot that you packed a gun in your luggage, and it was found, your new address would be Dog Hill Prison. And believe me, Chance, Dog Hill is not a place for a tall, slender, good-looking white boy from the big city."

"OK, I get it," I said. "In Balboa, only bad guys have guns, not poor businessmen who are only trying to protect themselves."

"Chance."

"Yes."

"I want you to hear me. No guns. Your blond hair, blue eyes, and infectious smile ain't going to save your white ass down here."

I sighed. "OK," I said. "I understand."

But as I left his office, I couldn't help but think, *Paul, old boy. No guns…you sure make me feel naked.*

Chapter Four

You know what luck is? Luck is believing you're lucky...to hold a
front position in this rat race, you've got to believe you're lucky.
—Stanley Kowalski in *A Streetcar Named Desire*

Leave it to a gaggle of lawyers and an overzealous government to take a problem that any third-grade student could understand and turn it into Einstein's theory of relativity. It had taken our consultants less than two months to determine that the resort was indeed a sleeping Caribbean jewel. But, just as I feared, our investigative work rekindled the interest of Diamond Resorts.

We had initially gained access to the site by virtue of a port-authority directive, but it hadn't taken long for Diamond Resorts to fire a torpedo across our bow by obtaining a court-ordered cease and desist injunction. Our lawyers believed that the port authority had the ultimate say, but we had to sit back and allow the courts to rule on the various motions.

Once we had determined that the King's Own deal might become a reality and that we were going to stay for some time, we brought our beautiful young daughter Rylee, and her grandmother Marilyn, down to San Vida. We were ecstatic to see them. Deb's mom lived in a separate suite at our home in the Old Mill area of West Toronto. More than just a grandmother, she was our babysitter, friend, and all-around go-to person whenever and wherever we needed her. She adored her granddaughter and we adored her.

So while the courts were doing their thing, we kicked back a bit, and the four of us spent some quality time enjoying and discovering the beautiful Caribbean. We flew over to Playas and, after a few days, sailed to the Bahamian island of Eleuthera and then finished our tour on the neighboring island of Abaco. Along the way we bought all the books we could find, and with the help of Wikipedia, we made a project of researching the history of the area. We all had heard the stories of the American rumrunners using the islands as staging areas back in the 1930s but had no idea about some of the rich lore that makes up the earlier Caribbean history. Surprisingly, we learned that the piracy of Captain Kidd, Edward Teach (better known as *Blackbeard*), Henry Morgan, Anne Bonny and Mary Read were often licensed by Spain or England or some other government to carry out their dirty work. But we were really dumfounded to learn that *wrecking* was a licensed profession in the Caribbean back in the day. Until the eighteen hundreds, the business of luring unsuspecting ships onto the coral reefs and islands was the main source of income for thousands. Once the ships had crashed and sunk, the wreckers would strip them of their cargo, and provided it wasn't too inconvenient, they might even save some of the crew and passengers.

Finally we returned home, and over a few glasses of wine, we couldn't help but ruefully joke about the parallels between then and now. Somebody even said, "Do you realize that the people who we are relying on to help us craft our deal to buy the resort, are the direct descendants of smugglers, pirates, and wreckers? So it will be interesting to see who's going to end up with the gold and who's going to crash on the rocks!" Everybody laughed—at least a little. But I was thinking, *Good point...and they've got home court advantage.*

Getting back to San Vida from our mini vacation meant getting back to work. The first stop was the corporate offices of the Balboan port authority to pick up some documents. While there, I struck up a conversation with one of the executives who happened to hail originally from Toronto. Ten years ago Ron Brady had come to Balboa for a vacation and just never left. He had met some guys at the Junkanoo Bar; one drink led to another, and soon he and nine of his new best friends decided to form a partnership to dive on sunken wrecks. His story was a little too much for me to accept initially, until I learned about the incredible number of shipwrecks in the area.

He was a very interesting guy with considerable local knowledge, so I suggested that we retire to the local pub to bond over a few beers. As the evening wore on, Ron explained that there were literally hundreds and hundreds of ships that had gone down in Caribbean waters over at least three centuries—victims of hurricanes, storms, and the ubiquitous coral reefs. I remained a little skeptical until he told me about the treasure of Lucaya.

A year or so before Ron arrived, a recreational swimmer went snorkeling and spearfishing about four hundred yards off the south shore of Grand Bahama Island. He came upon a galleon that had hit a coral reef hundreds of years earlier.

The diver and his buddies eventually reported $6 million in recovered treasure, although there was no way to verify how much may have been removed before prying eyes and poachers forced the treasure finders to make their findings public.

Unfortunately for Ron, his group never did hit a home run like the Lucayan treasure. So when the romance of trying to grind out a living by diving on old wrecks faded, he sold out, moved to Balboa, and went to work for the port authority.

We had a great evening telling war stories, and even though I killed far too many brain cells, I wouldn't soon forget what he told me, which included a couple of sidebars to my earlier travelling history lessons. It had never occurred to me, but there are no poisonous or dangerous creatures in the northern Caribbean. That is as long as you are on dry land, and as long as you're not on Grand Balboa Island. There are no poisonous snakes and no alligators like there are in Florida, which is only a few hundred miles away, and no crocodiles like those found in Central America. There are wild boars and wild horses on the island of Abaco, but as long as you don't bother them, they probably won't bother you.

"But," Ron said with a grin, "Grand Balboa Island has the sorry distinction of having about the worst kind of dangerous animal other than man—wild dogs that run in packs. Back in the seventies, many expatriates left the island due to the worldwide economic recession. Rather than take their dogs with them, many just took their animals out to the far east end of the island and dropped them off. Five became ten and ten became twenty, and before long, packs formed. With no natural predators and because the island residents don't have access to guns, the dogs found ways to survive and thrive."

"Creepy," I grimaced.

Ron laughed. "Oh, and that's not the half of it. A few years ago, a couple of thugs robbed a bank here in San Vida. They needed a getaway car, so they hijacked one. They drove it out to the east end of the island and tied the poor owner to a tree. They probably thought they were doing him a favor—instead of just shooting him, they gave him a chance. They assumed he'd get free or be found. And he was. By the dogs. Wasn't much left of him by the time he was discovered, still tied to the tree."

I greeted this story with stunned silence.

Ron nodded. "Must have been a terrible way to die."

With that unappetizing thought, a lovely young waitress came to take our orders. Both Ron and I watched her closely as she walked away. I figured it was always good to study the cultural offerings in a foreign land.

"Where was I?" he started. "Oh yeah. Back in the early thirties when US prohibition ended, the economy here went in the tank for a number of years. Eventually the scrub pine found here was recognized as having considerable value, and a major lumber industry developed. Around that time, US financier Walter Standing recognized the potential for tourism and business and hammered out an agreement with the Balboan government to introduce the concept of a 'free port' as a means of attracting commercial and industrial interests to Grand Balboa. As part of the process, Standing cut two brilliant deals that had far-reaching implications for the island. He convinced one of the world's wealthiest men, Daniel K. Bishop, to build a deep-water port. As part of their arrangement, Standing gave Bishop enough land to create the King's Own Resort and two beautiful championship golf courses.

"Once he had construction traction, Standing turned his attention to attracting North American tourists to Balboa. Casino gambling is always a great tourist amenity, so he turned the Mafia on to the opportunity. As with any enterprise, timing and luck can play a significant role, and as luck would have it, neighboring Havana, Cuba was being shut down by that upstart Fidel Castro. Mob boss Meyer Lansky et al, managed to ship much of their equipment and personnel to Balboa just before Castro closed the casinos and kicked all foreigners out of Cuba.

"So," Ron finished, "when you combine the proximity of Balboa to the United States and factor in the gambling, azure seas, sandy beaches, and soft tropic breezes, how could it miss? It was natural. Oh yeah, I forgot to mention—no state taxes, no federal taxes, no income tax. Really, how could it miss?"

Chapter Five

If my family lives for another hundred years, I want to live for
another one hundred years minus one day,
so I never have to live without them.
—Winnie the Pooh, as modified by Chance Daly

One Sunday morning shortly after my talk with Ron, I suggested to Debbie that we make an excursion out to the east end of the island. I had wisely mentioned absolutely nothing to her about the dogs and thus didn't have to worry about overcoming her innate maternal security system. I'm sure that if I had told her the gruesome story about the hijacked car owner, I'd never have been able to pry her or Rylee out of the car. As it was, I decided a local guide might be a good idea, so instead of driving our rental car, I figured we'd take a taxi, and that's how we met Hector. What a supercool dude.

I had driven down to the mall where I had noticed the cabbies hanging out and immediately spotted the cab for us. It was a minivan with a sign on the side that read, *$4.00 per head and the body goes free.* Of course, that price was just for rides inside the city, but with that come-on, who could resist?

While negotiating our fare, I brought up Ron's dog story. He said, "Yeah, mon. Der be dogs in de east end but nort side onlay. We gon sout side. I don like dogs anyway, so you be sure ain't none gon be round where we be goin."

Hector was a black guy, about eighty years old, five-foot-four, and at least three hundred pounds. I couldn't help but laugh to myself about that old joke: *If we do see the damn dogs, we don't need to outrun them. We only need to outrun you!*

Hector followed me home, and we quickly gathered the troops and jumped in his rattletrap van. Thoughtful Debbie had brought water for us all, as well as orange slices and some mango chunks. She shared everything with Hector and he instantly became part of the family. He was everything a three-hundred-pound guy is supposed to be—jovial to the core, and I think he knew everyone on the island.

For the first ten miles of paved road, we were introduced to one of the island's social niceties: every ten minutes or so, Hector would begin waving at an approaching car, and they would stop opposite each another to chat. Hector ignored the fact that two or three cars might have to stop behind them while he laughed and nattered back and forth about God knows what. Then they'd wave, and off we'd go again for another five miles, when he'd repeat the same scenario. Hector taught us that in Balboa, patience is not just a virtue but a necessity.

It was about twenty-five miles to the tip of the island, but we ran out of pavement after about fifteen miles. We ran out of pavement but not out of native settlements. We were going fairly slow on the packed coral and sand road anyway, but we slowed down even more when we drove through the tiny Balboan villages. Our timing was perfect. Inching along, we were thrilled to hear the church congregations singing their hearts out as only the Baptists seem to do. It was uplifting, although it made me feel a little guilty about not going to church as often as I knew Father Anthony and my mom would have wished.

The best thing about having Hector as a driver was that he not only knew everybody but also seemed to know all sorts of fun facts. Every cove and inlet prompted another history lesson about everything from pirates to smugglers. We were reminded that Sir Francis Drake would have sailed by here, as did the famed explorer Balboa, who was the first European to discover the Pacific Ocean. Eventually the sandy road took us to the end of the island, which also terminated the ridge. We got out of the car and wandered up to the top of the ridge, only to be surprised to find the ruins of an old fort from the 1700s. Most of the walls had crumbled, but seven cannon barrels still pointed majestically out to the northern Caribbean. I wanted to keep exploring, but Hector wouldn't have any of it. Even at gunpoint, I couldn't have made him go any farther.

"No, mon. Ain't goin no furtha. Dey be dogs furtha. Ain't goin!"

Unfortunately for me, Debbie overheard him, interrogated him, and that quickly brought an end to our excursion and an abrupt halt to my idea of searching for pirate treasure, jewelry, and pieces of eight.

Prodded by an annoyed Debbie, we scampered back to the van. Even though I correctly pointed out that we hadn't even heard, let alone seen a dog, my defense fell on deaf ears. As far as she was concerned, I had placed her family in harm's way. I made a mental note to reduce Hector's tip.

Once we were safely in the van and in an effort to change subjects and to get Debbie off my back, I asked Hector why on earth anyone would build a fort at that particular location. He explained that not only were there large gaps in the coral reefs that allowed ships to get close to shore, but the fort was built to lay claim to, and to control, a large freshwater spring.

"Wow," I said as the commercial possibility came to me in a flash. That meant that any ship looking to stock up had to deal with the "owners" of the spring. My imagination took over, and I could envision battles fought and deals struck over this incredibly valuable commodity. I shared my entrepreneurial thoughts with Debbie, but it still took about fifteen minutes of my blathering to warm up the interior of the van.

Chapter Six

Somewhere the dice are in the air.
Cards are being shuffled.
Someone is saying, "Shut up and deal."
—J. B. Beatty

It's hard to believe that a place with so many positive things going for it could get so screwed up. But all it took was some belligerent labor-union executives, the rising tide of black power seeking revenge from real or imagined historical prejudices, and a couple of back-to-back hurricanes, and the economy of Balboa was like air slowly leaking out of a tire.

First one expat left with a bad taste in his mouth, and then another, and then the exodus gathered momentum, culminating in a slew of abandoned houses and closed businesses. And to exacerbate the situation, the void was prime to be filled by the drug culture.

But that was ancient history. And now the more I looked, the more emotionally committed I became. Maybe this was the real deal. All I had to do was wait for the government to do their legislative thing and hope they could bash Diamond Resorts onside. And in the meantime, what to do?

Playing golf was always a good option for me. Until the two King's Own golf courses were reopened, there was only one other course on the island. The Balboa G&C was a nice track carved out of the pines and designed by Jack Nicklaus. But even better, I soon learned that there was lots of live action with the regulars. They had an active men's league playing every Wednesday, and in addition, every day, rain or shine, at least ten guys showed up to play cards, with Gin or Hearts usually being the game du jour. I thought I may have died and gone to heaven. That's not to say these guys were easy pickings. They weren't. But none of them were hurting for a buck and they would all bet on anything and everything at any time.

Once it got around that I was buying the King's Own, I was established as bona fide and could get a golf game or card game any time I wanted. In my youth, I had hung out in the pool room at the Liberty bowling alley in West Toronto. Substitute this golf course for that pool room and this was like a homecoming. The cast of characters was different, but the culture was the same. Even the hours were the same: every day at two o'clock, rain or shine, a game of Hearts or Gin broke out in the clubhouse. And I liked their overall attitude. The first guy I met at the course told me that he had made his first two-dollar bet when he was fifteen. He said he had lost it and had spent the last forty years and about two million dollars trying to win it back.

Most of these guys had money, and gambling was their entertainment, and an essential part of their lifestyle. They would typically play *something* until about five, at which time they would drift off to wives, girlfriends, whatever. And one night a week, they would be back for a poker game. It was open to anybody. As a result the drinking, the old boy camaraderie, and the ton of cash on the table created great opportunities for any cheater, grifter, or crossroader who happened to be in Balboa and who had found out about the game.

With an uncharacteristic caution, I had decided that until I knew who was doing what to whom, I'd play, but I'd run silent and run deep. I'd play for small stakes, and for once in my life, I'd try to keep my mouth shut.

Within a couple of weeks, I had spotted some scams and had a pretty good handle on who the cheaters were. Being the new kid on the block, however, I had to endure the splashing performances. "Splashing" is a hustler's term that means throwing money around by foolish betting. It's geared to make a mark relax. Some scammers can pull it off naturally, but having seen it all before, some of these guys stuck out like hookers teaching Sunday school. In my first poker game I quickly put the scammers at ease. I raised when I should have folded a couple of times and then showed my cards when I bluffed, like only a buffoon would do. After my several-week acting performance, which might have been worthy of an Oscar, the regulars dropped their guard, and I started doing pretty well. But as discretion is the better part of valor, I decided that I wouldn't clean out the game anytime soon. I enjoyed the regular outings with the guys and didn't want to spoil it.

The poker games were one thing, but the afternoon Gin games gave me heartburn. Sometimes identifying one problem can lead to another even larger problem, and while hanging out and kibitzing at some of the Gin games, I saw some stuff that stuck in my craw. But what the hell was I going to do with the information? It had taken about a *New York minute* to spot the gaffs, but now what?

My problem was that the heaviest loser in the game was the one guy that I had been tipped off about. He was being ripped off by some guys who were pretending to be his best buddies. I hate that. It's one thing to cheat, but my sense of righteous indignation was in full bloom once I saw him being taken to the cleaners by guys pretending to be his friends. Soft-spoken, unassuming, and slight, seventy-year-old Sy Goldstein seemed downright grandfatherly. Except for the eyes. His eyes were completely blank. He might have felt real emotion—although there's no proof that he did—but he never showed it. He was impossible to read.

Sy was a transplanted New Yorker who appeared in San Vida around 2000. I had heard rumors that he was a hit man, although nobody could confirm that. But I could believe it. He was always calm, almost serene, but you could feel that right under the surface, he was coiled tight as a drum. You knew he could go off at any second.

The scoop on Sy was that he was always around until you realized he wasn't. He never said where or when he was going, and never said where he had been. But a few times a year, people would notice that he hadn't been seen around the golf club for a few weeks. Then he'd be back, with no hint or acknowledgment that he'd even been gone.

Sy never caused any trouble, and I didn't want anything I did to upset the aquarium. Once my suspicions were confirmed, I had a dilemma. I knew that Sy was often the heavy loser at Gin. I also knew full well that if I didn't tell him what I knew as soon as I knew it, my tardiness could conceivably be injurious to my health. So I sucked it up, took him aside, and told him over a beer that he was being cheated. First, I told him what I was about to tell him. Then I told him. And then I told him what I had just told him. I had to. I had to say it three times because the first two times, there was no reaction—none. He just looked at me. Or actually, he looked right through me.

Finally, skeptical but interested, he asked, "You sure? How are they doing it?"

I gulped and plowed on, "Marked cards. The club provides playing cards made by Bees Manufacturing."

"So?"

I continued. "The cards have that tiny diamond design on the back. Get a deck and riffle through them. You'll see that the half diamonds along the edges will often jump back and forth. Sometimes they're not uniform. When manufacturing a deck of cards, the complete fifty-two cards are supposed to be cut from the same sheet. That way, all the edges are absolutely the same. But scammers will buy multiple cases of decks and assemble a deck of sorts. Sorts are the cards that are cut from decks slightly off center. The cheater removes the high-valued cards from an off-center deck and mixes them with the low-valued cards from a regular deck. And that's all he needs to do. He can spot the high-value cards from a mile away. This gives him a huge edge in any Gin game."

"Do you know who's doing it?"

"Shouldn't be hard to figure out," I said. "Who wins the least often but wins the most money when they do win?"

"Jeff," he said. "Jeff and Nicky. When you play them one on one, they can be beat. But when they play as partners, they're double tough."

"Sy," I said. "I've been a little reluctant to say anything because I don't have a dog in the fight. As the new kid on the block, I would normally just live and let live. But you seem like a good guy, and I hate like hell to see you get taken down by guys who are pretending to be your friends. That's cold."

He said nothing. I took a sip of my beer and searched his eyes for a response. Blank. Finally, I asked, "How much do you figure you've lost to those weasels?"

Sy thought about it for a long time. Finally, he said, "Maybe about twenty thousand, maybe thirty thousand over the last six months or so. Why?"

"Well, I think I might have a plan that would help you get even."

"I'm all ears," he growled.

"Let's take them down." I laughed a little nervously, remembering Sy's supposed profession. "I don't mean take them out. Let's just give them a taste of their own medicine."

"How?"

"A freeze-out game. Tell you what—why don't you come over to my house and we can talk without anybody walking in on us? I'd like you to meet my family anyway."

Sy came over later that afternoon and met Debbie, Marilyn, and our munchkin, Rylee. Debbie had just been next door visiting the neighbors, and she certainly broke the ice with Sy when she told us about her visit. She said they appeared to be nice, normal, quiet, forty-year-old folks with a couple of nice, normal, teenage sons. And they have four nice, quiet, golden Labrador Retrievers. They also have a parrot that was not so nice. Debbie said that the parrot sat on his perch the entire time she was there, and every few minutes it would say, "Awk... FUCK OFF!" Debbie said our neighbors appeared not to even hear it.

Sy choked on his drink.

Following Debbie's icebreaker, Sy and I retired to the patio, and I laid out my plan. It was fairly simple, and I loved the fact that they would never even know that we were using cheating methods to take them down. "Sy," I said, "if we play our cards right, so to speak, they won't even know what hit them. Turnabout's fair play! Right? But the key will be for you to get them locked into a four-handed Gin game with no escape. Up north we used to call it a freeze-out game. Each player puts up a predetermined amount, say twenty-five thousand dollars, and the game isn't over until one team loses their fifty thousand."

"How do we know we're gonna win?" Sy asked.

"That's the easy part. But can you get them into a game?"

"Damn right I can. They think I'm going senile anyway, and after the way you've been playing poker with us, the word's around that you've got more money than brains. Shit, if I suggest a game with a fifty-thousand-dollar brass ring, they'll send limos to pick us up. But how are we going to beat them?"

"Sy, my boy, we've got a lot of things going for us. First of all, they haven't got a clue that we're onto them. So all we've got to do is get our own gaffed readers into the game at the right time. I'll make up some decks of sorted Bees with just a couple of 'mistakes' on the backs—mismarked so that when they think the marking is a high card, it will actually be a low denomination. And for good measure, I'll daub the cards."

"What the hell does that mean?" asked Sy.

"I can get some marking ink over here in about two days. The ink can only be detected through special lenses—it's absolutely invisible to the naked eye. I'll mark our newly gaffed Bees so that only you and I will be able to see and read them through our lenses. You wear glasses anyway, and I can have a pair doctored for you, so no problem. And I'll get some contact lenses to wear. With those special lenses, my markings will stand out like neon signs. The only trick is going to be getting our deck into the game, and even that won't be difficult. I know where the club keeps the inventory of cards and chips, so I'll just get into that cabinet and substitute our marked decks for theirs, and that's about all the help we'll need."

After he left, I wondered if this had been the first time he'd been invited into anyone's home as a guest. You could see that he absolutely relished being with us in our casa. That one invitation became the basis of a tight relationship, and I knew from that day forth that I could take that bond to the bank regardless of the results of our upcoming Gin game.

Over the next few days, I hung out and kibitzed a bit in the men's game room while watching a few of Jeff and Nicky's Gin games. Over a drink at the club with Sy a few days before we took them on, I told him that I had noticed another way that they were cheating, and that we might be able to take advantage of it.

"Sy," I began, "watch the way those guys pick up the cards at the end of the hand. When they deal, they often stack the deck."

"How?" asked Sy.

"When picking up the cards after a hand, they will occasionally keep a run intact—say the four, five, six, and seven of hearts. Or they'll pick up a meld of say, four kings, and place it on the bottom of the deck. Then they keep them on the bottom by shuffling only the cards above them. It's not hard to do and unless somebody is watching for it specifically, most people would never notice. Then just before they offer the cards to be cut, they cut about fifteen cards off and place them on the bottom of the deck as part of the final shuffle. Then they offer the deck to be cut. They know that most people cut the cards about in the middle, so when the cards are cut, the cheats know the approximate location of the four cards. They then deal the cards as usual and will automatically be dealing two of the cards to themselves and two to their opponent. At that point they know two of the cards in their opponent's hand, which gives them a huge advantage. If they're ten-count cards, they can wait you out. As the hand progresses, most people get nervous about having twenty points in their hand late in the game, so they're likely to start discarding the high cards. It works the same with the four-card run. As soon as they see that they've been dealt two of the run, they know that you have the other two."

"So what should I do about it?" asked Sy.

"Well, there are a couple of things we can do. We can either play offense or defense. And don't forget we have an edge. They don't know that we know, what they're doing, so *maybe* we can use that to our advantage. One of the things we could do defensively would be to employ the Scarne cut. In fact, it's a good habit to get into using that cut anytime you play cards."

"How do you do it?"

"Well, I'll tell you, but for this game, let's not tip them off by using it. We're in good shape with our daubed cards, so let's not do anything to wake them up. It's fairly simple. Most people cut about half the deck off the top and put the bottom half on top, right?"

"Right."

"Well, instead of doing that, lift off the top ten to fifteen cards with the left hand, and then with the right hand, lift off half of the remaining cards and put the fifteen cards that were first cut on top of the cards remaining on the table and put this last group on top of those. So essentially, you've broken the deck into three parts instead of two. I even go a step further by breaking the process into four or five sections. By the time I get through with my modified Scarne cut, most mechanics are so confused that they lose track of where their cheating cards are. It's effective, believe me.

"But that's defense, and like I said, let's not do that in our game. We don't want to tip them off. An offensive maneuver we can employ is to use what we know about the cards they have in their hands. If you see a guy playing with the discards, and he subsequently gives you a pair of ten counts, the odds are pretty good that he has the other two ten counts. If that's the case, use that knowledge to your advantage. Try to tie up the two cards he needs by employing them in runs in your hand. If you can do that, you've accomplished two things—not only have you locked up the two cards that he needs to make his hand, but you've also saddled him with a twenty-point count in the event that you Gin or knock."

After my dissertation, Sy was double pumped. It only took a few days for him to put together the game. We had it set for the following Friday at one o'clock, and by the time I got there around twelve thirty, our game had drawn a bit of a crowd. Incredibly, there was hardly any room left. Even a few gals showed up, wanting to watch the action, but they were turned away by some brave bachelors who correctly pointed out that the game was taking place in an ante room just off the men's locker room. Ergo, women could not be accommodated in good conscience. Sy and I took our seats at the table, and within minutes our opponents arrived just oozing with confidence. One of the pricks was dressed in typical country-club garb, looking as if he had just stepped out of *GQ* magazine. The other dink not so much. He looked like a pimp going to a whore's wedding, or maybe to a disco, rather than to his own funeral. It was good though; it gave me a couple more good reasons to dislike them.

It was a bit of a gong show at the beginning. Each player had to pony up their $25,000 in cash, which was in turn, counted by a member of the other team. We decided that rather than leave the cash just lying around, we would put it in the golf-club safe. A good idea to be sure, but I was also happy to see that Greg Goodkey, the top cop on the island, was there watching the action as well. His sizable presence alone commanded respect. It was also comforting to know that he was the only police officer in all of Balboa who was allowed to carry a gun. This major government concession was direct acknowledgment that he had made serious enemies of a lot of bad people over the years. It probably also had something to do with the fact he was the only white senior police officer in all of Balboa. Talk about having a bullseye on your back!

There was only a slight delay while the eight decks of "new cards" were retrieved from the club cabinet and dropped on the table. As I appeared to be inspecting the cellophane on the boxes (which I had carefully replaced once I had marked the cards), Sy—bless his tiny "larcenous" heart—got up from the table and announced to the standing-room crowd that he was taking side action. While all this was going on, I pretended to be dumfounded by his antics and even protested weakly that we already had enough exposure. And I must have done a hell of an acting job because the odds against us kept going up, and I'd be damned if he didn't end up taking another $8,000 in bets, with the last $2,000 having us as two-to-one underdogs. Knowing that we were about to cheat the cheaters, I didn't like that idea at all, but what the hell was I going to say to Sy, except "Let's cut for deal and let's get it on"!

At the outset of our little charade, I had been somewhat concerned that Sy might be the weaker member of our team. But no, he was the perfect partner. The game went down as smooth as silk. We got their $50,000. Sy made his tall dollars in side bets. The bad guys got heartburn.

Chapter Seven

My favorite poker chip trick is to make everyone's chips disappear.
—Amarillo Slim

While all this was going on, I was making plans to get the resort open. It looked like it was all coming together, with both the government and Diamond Resorts making sounds like they wanted to do a deal. Debbie had found her niche as well and began volunteering at Mary Star of the Sea School. She found it fun and fulfilling and soon developed a close friendship with another volunteer mother, Maria Diego.

"Maria Diego?" I said. "You're kidding. She's Raymundo's wife. Do you know who he is?"

Sy had told me a little about Raymundo. I knew that he was referred to as Padrino by his bodyguard. But before I had any inkling about what a really bad dude he was, I had taken a grand off him with some proposition bets during one of our weekly Texas Hold'em games at the golf club. It had been a dull game and a boring night, so to crank up a little action I said, "On the next deal, I'll bet anyone that a face card will appear on the flop."

Raymundo said, "I'll bet you a C-note that one doesn't."

Sure enough, the jack of hearts came up on the flop.

Raymundo slipped a hundred-dollar bill across the table to me. "Let's go again," he said. "Two hundred this time."

Queen of hearts.

One of the players said, "He's scamming you, Raymundo."

"Shut up!" Raymundo snapped. He looked hard at me. "A grand," he said.

Now I was the guy with the problem. How to shut this off? I said, "OK, but this is the last bet. I'm not going to let you double and double."

The dealer dealt the card. I was almost afraid to look. *King of spades.*

He pulled out his wallet and slapped ten one hundred dollar bills onto the table. He was scowling but didn't say a word.

I didn't mind the color of his money, but I didn't like that he had become the butt of all the jokes. So in an attempt to cool him down, as I picked up his C-notes with my one hand, I tossed back the first $300 I had won with my other hand. Luckily for me, he had given me the $1,000 without any problem, but you could see he was really steamed. He felt he had been ambushed, and, of course he had. I'd had about a 10 percent edge, and if I had let the betting continue long enough, I would have eventually won his new Cadillac. But I stopped it before he got hit too badly. It was the right call. Because while my bet was with Raymundo, I could not shake the penetrating gaze that I was getting from the tall, thin, immaculately attired goon standing ten feet behind him. His bodyguard took his job far too seriously for my liking.

Raymundo played a lot of poker with us, and as far as I know, nobody ever saw his guy, Marco, leave his side. They were like a pair of nuns: always together. Behind their backs the running joke was, "Let's keep Raymundo happy and coming back. Maybe we should let him win a little something every week. When he's here, he's our best insurance against getting robbed." But that was easier said than done. Raymundo had enough money to retire the country's national debt, but he needed a way to find gratification with all his wealth, and poker and coke were his passions. Unfortunately for him, he just wasn't very good at either.

Out on the driving range the day after my encounter with Raymundo, Sy gave me some information that I wished he had told me before I'd gotten cross threaded with him. It turned out that the Colombian was about sixty, with big league money and a nasty drug habit. He had married Maria, a former Miss Colombia, about seven years ago, and they had a cute little girl about Rylee's age. Evidently, Raymundo had been one of the first drug cartel guys to pioneer the use of the northern Bahamas for smuggling marijuana and cocaine into the United States in the 1990s.

An associate of his, Carlos Ledher, had built on the Bahamian drug smuggling legacy and had moved his operation to the small island of Norman Cay. First he bought a home and then added to his property holdings, and with the help of corrupt Bahamian Prime Minister Lynden Pindling, he pushed out the locals and created a fiefdom. Norman Cay eventually boasted its own airport, docks, wharfs, fleets of airplanes and boats, and an entire infrastructure whose sole purpose was to support the smuggling of vast amounts of drugs into the United States. The Medellin cartel that he represented was so successful that he helped make the leader, Pablo Escobar, the seventh wealthiest person in the world at the time. There was no telling how much money they made, but to put it in perspective, the American DEA caught Pindling taking a $56 million bribe.

But clever Raymundo skated before the collapse of the Norman Cay operation. He was already long gone to Grand Balboa, and while Ledher was doing his thing, Raymundo wisely stayed under the radar. San Vida was his sanctuary, and he did everything prudent to keep a low profile, with the exception of the mansion he had built just east of the Balboa Beach Hotel. It was about ten thousand square feet and had three casitas. But the size of the main house wasn't too different from that of his neighbors. There were a number of wealthy expats who had even larger homes in the gated community, so his didn't stand out. The only really unusual feature was that he had carved his own channel through the coral reef that protected the beach and then further chopped his channel across the beach another five hundred feet into his compound, where he parked his two thirty-foot cigarette, ocean-friendly racing boats in his state-of-the-art boathouse. His estate was protected by an array of cameras. The most dominant architectural feature was the twelve-foot wall topped by glass shards and barbed wire.

Sy also shared a brief story about Raymundo's sidekick, Marco. Legend has it that Raymundo was hosting a "business" meeting on a sixty-foot yacht that he had brought over from Miami for the occasion. Those in attendance included drug lords from Colombia, Mexico, and South Florida. They were moored about a mile offshore on a typically beautiful Balboan day with blue skies and temperatures in the eighties.

But the tranquility was being shattered by a guy on a wave runner. He kept circling the yacht, showing off, and ogling the nude gals who were stretched out sunbathing on the decks. The noise apparently irritated Raymundo, who ordered Marco to tell the guy that he was spoiling an otherwise lovely day and to ask him to please take his noisy machine elsewhere. The guy ignored Marco's request, which was a discourteous and a really ignorant thing to do. In retrospect it would even be classified as a mistake.

As he circled the yacht again, Marco disappeared and quickly came up from the galley with a six-pack of Heineken. He shouted to the wave-runner dude and pointed to the beer indicating that he would give it to him if he would take his loud obnoxious machine and move out of earshot. Who could resist cold Heinekens on such a hot day? Wave-runner guy sure couldn't.

That was his second mistake. As he came along side and reached for the beer, Marco shot him right between the eyes. Lines were quickly thrown around former surfer dude and his wave runner. The yacht engine was engaged, and a slow-moving procession was driven five more miles out to the Atlantic. The entire matter only took thirty minutes, and neither the wave runner nor the guy were ever seen again. And the meeting in the stateroom? It went on, with none of the participants even knowing what had happened. All Padrino knew was that the noise had stopped, just as he had requested.

Despite my misgivings, Debbie told me that she had already arranged with Maria for the four of us to go out to dinner. We were to meet them at their house the following night.

The place looked like a palace. Or maybe a fortress. *All it needs is a moat*, I thought. There were video cameras mounted on the brick columns that supported the huge iron gate. I smiled into one of the cameras and told it that Chance and Debbie had arrived. After about five seconds, the gate slowly swung open, and we drove up the long cobblestone driveway.

We were greeted at the door by a uniformed maid who politely guided us through a very sophisticated metal detector: the kind only airports could afford.

Once it was established that Debbie and I weren't carrying weapons, we were allowed into the living room, where we were greeted warmly by Maria and politely by Raymundo.

Maria smiled brightly and said, "Would you like the fifty-cent tour?"

Debbie looked thrilled. She hadn't fooled me. I was sure this was her prime motivation from the start.

Their home was not quite as big as the Taj Mahal, but we both walked through it like a couple of country rubes on their first visit to the big city. I had hung out with some high rollers in my time and I'd been in many a lavish mansion, but this made the best of them look like studio apartments. While we toured, we encountered a couple of guys watching a bank of monitors that showed every angle of the front and back yards. Several other men were snacking in the kitchen or just hanging out. They clearly all played on the same team because they all wore identical uniforms: tailored navy blue pants, fitted white shirts, and shoulder holsters with the cutest matching 45s. The scene was right out of a *Godfather* movie.

But even though this collection of goons made me a little nervous, I couldn't help but be impressed. It wasn't just the furnishings and design of the mansion. It was the high-tech security, surveillance, and communication center that blew me away. The compound even had its own generator that would kick in when the power went out, a common occurrence in San Vida.

After our tour, Marco drove the four of us to the Stoned Crab, a restaurant famous throughout the Caribbean and not just for its excellent seafood. Built immediately adjacent to the harbor with parking at the front, and the dining room and bar at the rear, the restaurant was open to an incredible view of the boats in the marina on one side and the ships in the harbor on the other. But the pièce de résistance was the outdoor patio that extended about thirty feet over the water. The floor was made of clear tempered glass. Seated diners could see straight down to watch the water lap against the pilings. Until they rang the gong.

At 8:00 p.m., chefs, waiters, and busboys formed a procession, marching from the kitchen out to the railing, accompanied musically by the *Jaws* theme. With considerable drama, they carried platters of table scraps, carcasses, and kitchen leftovers to a specific spot on the tempered glass. Then, with great fanfare, the chef climbed onto a short platform and began to hit a metal gong.

Within seconds the ocean beneath the feet of those gathered on the transparent floor became a broiling cauldron of writhing, ferocious sharks, the largest of which was an enormous eighteen-foot white shark. Leaping upward and crashing back into their horrible counterparts, they fought and tore into the meat and bones being dropped over the side. I don't know about everyone else, but I had nightmares for weeks. Occasionally I still do.

Other than the shark episode (which was in a different category altogether) and the show of military might at the Diego fortress, it was as pleasant an evening as one could expect, considering the fact that we were dining with a drug lord who had sampled too much of his own wares. In fact, in some weird way, the shark-feeding frenzy became a bit of a bonding experience. It gave us a common topic and provided considerable fodder whenever the conversation lagged, which wasn't often.

Debbie could carry on a conversation with a lamp post, and once Maria got over her initial shyness, she too entered into the conversational fray, so much so that Raymundo and I could hardly get a word in edgewise. Soon he and I and the ever-present Marco drifted over to the bar for an after-dinner Grand Marnier. The girls, being in full yap, didn't miss us for a heartbeat. It turned out that Raymundo was a buddy of Marc Anthony, Jennifer Lopez's ex-husband, who owned a piece of the Miami Dolphins. As such, he was a big Dolphins fan, and between injury-report discussions and point-spread considerations, we speculated on the outcome of the upcoming weekend's football games.

Eventually the girls came looking for us and during the ride home, Debbie, with all the subtlety of a sledgehammer, told us that next week was the annual Mary Star of the Sea School outdoor fair and charity church bazaar and that she expected *both* of us to not only donate three prizes each for bingo but also that we were to sell bingo cards. I would never have believed it, but Raymundo meekly agreed and even asked what time she would like him to show up.

The church bazaar was one of the more popular events on the Balboa residents' social calendar. Debbie and Maria headed out early in the morning to help organize the booths, tables, and tents. I arrived about an hour or so later and was pleased to see that the entire church parking lot and lawn were so packed with cars that I had to drive a fair distance down the road just to find a parking space. Walking back, I could see that a great crowd was already milling among the many vendors and displays that were offering food, games, and the always popular kids' fishing well, ringed with munchkins trying to hook numbered plastic ducks. It was neat. The kids looked very determined to win those brightly colored five-cent ribbon bows that little girls so proudly wear.

I steered my way through the milling crowd, clutching three brand-new iPads, all the while looking out for Raymundo. We had previously agreed to meet near the front entrance of the church, but he wasn't there. I recognized and acknowledged a number of guys from the golf club and was pleasantly surprised to see that the event appeared to have attracted a fair number of camera-clutching tourists as well. While scanning the farthest corner of the yard, I saw—or for a second, *thought* I saw—a familiar figure from days long past. He was leaning against a large Eucalyptus tree, but he had turned and walked away before I could even process the thought.

Could that be? Nah, I knew it was a stupid idea. That guy was long out of my life, and anyway, the resemblance hadn't even been that close. Just then I felt a hand on my shoulder. "It seems that great minds think alike." I turned to see Raymundo peering down into my paper bag containing the three iPads. We each had brought the same prizes for bingo. We laughed, and I said, "The girls are going to be thrilled. Shit, even I'd consider playing bingo for the chance to win one of these babies." We both laughed again. "Let's go find them. Bingo starts at noon, and I'm sure Debbie is anxious to announce what the prizes are going to be." We pushed through the crowd toward the church entrance.

Later that night, relaxing over a glass of wine, Debbie told me how happy she was with the results of the charity bazaar and more specifically, how grateful she was for my help. She finally said, "When we were cleaning up the grounds, I managed to get around and thank all the volunteers. The only one I didn't thank was you. Now it's your turn. Let's go to bed."

Moonlit Caribbean night. Soft, gentle breeze. The smell of orchids in the air. Beautiful woman. Sometimes I'm really, really glad I'm me.

Chapter Eight

Our role in life sometimes seems preordained.
Can we change who we are? Can we alter our destiny?
—Seymour Harris, Rancho Mirage, California

Unfortunately, the mellow, civilian life wasn't to last. Raymundo may have been a good charity volunteer, but within weeks he was involved in a situation that reminded us that a leopard doesn't change his spots.

There was a Kentucky Fried Chicken (KFC) at the Y intersection on Queen's Highway heading out of San Vida. Swing to the left and the road took you to the east side of the harbor where the Stoned Crab Restaurant was located. Swing to the right and it took you west, by the native town of Ten Mile Rock and eventually to West End, which had been a primary embarkation point back in the rum-running days in the 1920s. The KFC was perfectly situated because the Y catches everyone coming and going both to and from "The Rock." But it was busy not just because they sold good chicken: they also sold weed from the take-out window.

This drive-through amenity was appreciated by just about everybody except Raymundo. He didn't have a problem with them selling grass—the problem was that they had stopped buying their supply from his operation. The KFC action was small potatoes for Raymundo, but he liked to keep his fingers in the business, and after all, he had been selling them product in bulk quantities at wholesale prices for a long time. But greed must have set in, and at some point the KFC clowns decided to cut out the middleman. To Raymundo, this was disrespectful. It was also a very bad idea.

Raymundo's initial response to this transgression had occurred just before we got to the island. One night after closing, in an attempt to get the proprietor's attention, Raymundo's crew took a few sticks of dynamite and simply blew up the KFC kitchen. Not much drama in and of itself. The owner, however, must have been a slow learner because he not only took his insurance proceeds and rebuilt his kitchen, but he also added another two thousand square feet onto his restaurant, and he *still* refused to buy his weed from Raymundo. The only thing he did that showed any semblance of intelligence was installing a nine-foot-high barbed wire fence around the new premises. He also had San Vida Canine Services deliver three German Shepherd guard dogs each night at closing time. Evidently, this annoyed Raymundo even more. In fact, it was like waving a red flag in front of a charging bull.

Six months later, about 7:00 a.m., the canine company picked up their patrol dogs right on schedule. And wouldn't you know it, shortly before the morning staff arrived at eight, *someone* used enough dynamite to blow the new building into orbit. We lived six miles away, and the explosion shook us awake, along with every resident in San Vida. Evidently, insurance companies are reluctant to insure a twice-blown-up building for a third time, which is why, to this day, there is no Kentucky Fried Chicken in San Vida.

The guys around the golf club had known that Raymundo was cranky with his former customer, so we occasionally gave him a bit of a hard time about the shortage of good take-out chicken on the island. But it was all in good humor. Raymundo just smiled and suggested that we consider going to McDonald's. Marco smiled, too—just a little.

Chapter Nine

If you tell me who your friends are, I'll tell you your future.
—Rodrigues Farias, Cullican, Mexico

There was a bit of a lull in all our activities, so Debbie and I decided to spend some quality family time together. Norm wasn't around—he had announced that he might go over to Miami to do some shopping. I immediately thought that the real reason he was stateside was to hook up with that airline stewardess he had met on the way down. But he said no, that he wanted to "do some shopping, take in some jai alai, and watch a few greyhounds chase a rabbit around a race track."

I told Debbie about Norm's plan and suggested that maybe we should go too. She quickly put a kibosh on that idea. "Norm's got something else going on. He doesn't shop. He buys. The only time he goes into a mall is to see a movie. You're staying home with me. I'll find fun things for you to do."

As usual, she was right.

Three days later, Norm came to our front door, and I heard, "Chance, we need to talk." No *hello* or *how are you?* or *what's going on?* None of that: simply, "Chance, we need to talk."

"Norm, you always make me nervous when you say that. OK, grab a beer from the fridge. Let's go out to the patio."

As we sat down under the umbrella, he started somewhat sheepishly, "Well…you know I've been over in Miami doing a little shopping, and while there I met up with some of our old friends. I knew at least a couple of them were coming down, so I took the opportunity to visit. Also ever since we came to San Vida, I've been feeling only partially dressed, so I thought it might be an idea to pick up some accessories. Nothing serious, you understand. Just some small pieces—a couple of minor-league handguns and a shotgun. Rather like security blankets, you might say. This morning I dropped by and saw Debbie. You guys now have one stashed in the base of the big lamp on your bedside table. Also, your car and van each have a new false bottom in the middle consoles. There's a piece in each. Also, there will be one in the safe at your house. Oh yeah, maybe I didn't mention that? I've ordered you a safe as well. It should be here next week. I thought we'd sink it in concrete under the barbecue."

Not really surprised by Norm's actions, I nevertheless blurted out, "But we don't have a barbecue."

"And that's another thing. I bought you a barbecue. It will be here next week, as well."

"OK, got it. But before you get into why you're really here, how was the jai alai?"

"It was ok. I didn't lose too much But it's easier to pick a broken nose than it is to pick a winner at that game" Norm said ruefully.

"Got it. Now what's up?"

"As you know, I've been staying in contact with our old buddy, Country. He's been anxious to visit. Says he needs to get away from his future ex-wife. Apparently she's mad at him again. He said that recently he asked her what she would do if he won the lottery. She said, 'I'd take half and leave you.' Then he said he made the mistake of saying, 'Well, I just won twelve bucks, so here's six dollars. Now get lost!"

I stifled a laugh because I knew Norm was about to drop the other shoe.

"Anyway, when I saw Country, I also saw a couple of our old friends. Father Anthony was there, and it was great to see him. But Johnny A. was there, too. I know, I know, but honestly I didn't put it together until I got to the jai alai game and saw the three of them waiting for me. It was awesome to see Father Anthony. He still has his finger in our old Churches in Action Casino and says it continues to pay off like a charity wishing well. Country was a little quiet at first but not Johnny. Johnny was still Johnny. Big brass balls. By the way, Country says he's cutting back on his drinking. He said he has been sober now for forty-nine days. Not in a row, mind you, but he says it's a start."

Our friend Country was a guy who always dressed like a cowboy, Smith Bilt Stetson hat and all. He had hung out with us ever since our days at the Liberty Bowling Alley in West Toronto. He was a hoot. Called everybody "Cuz" and talked in parables. He had more lines than the telephone company and was always complaining about Jackie, his long-suffering wife. He said recently he thought she had died. He said the sex was the same, but the ironing was piling up.

But Johnny Andrews was there. That was a surprise. Johnny A., "Angles," was one of my best friends growing up—a super guy to hang with and certainly the brightest of us all. We chased girls, shot Craps, chased girls, played cards, chased girls, and worked more proposition bets than Titanic Thompson. He was also my second-in-command at our barely legal CIA club in Toronto and had conjured up our motto: Building a Better Community through Charity and Understanding. Johnny had it all. Tall, slim, good-looking, great athlete. But as bright as he was, Johnny just couldn't play by the rules all the time. He always had to *bend*, twist, slip, or slide. He epitomized the old line: *"If you don't cheat and you lose, you've got only yourself to blame."*

We had always tolerated Johnny's indiscretions in our younger days. He was so bright, so full of energy, and it was super exciting having him around. However, we always had to worry just a little about getting contaminated by some of his escapades. But at the time, we thought we were young, nine feet tall, and bulletproof, and nobody could tell us anything about anything.

As Johnny and the rest of us grew into our twenties, moving our floating Craps and poker games to different hotel conference rooms and service-club halls every week, became old and tedious. I had come up with the idea of seeing if Father Anthony would throw his church's support behind a permanent charity casino. He didn't even have to pray for guidance— he saw the potential immediately. Once he was on board, we applied for a gaming-exemption license based on his church's charitable endeavor, and we were off to the races. We were blessed from the beginning.

Father Anthony was a great guy to work with and any time a visiting councilman, politician, or even a policeman came around for a look-see, a quick call to Father A. would have him over to the CIA club in a heartbeat. He'd conduct the tour, always asking everyone to join him in a brief prayer as they were leaving the club. No wonder we were so successful. We had a great idea, treated everyone fairly and honestly, and with Father Anthony's help, we always felt we had the big guy upstairs looking out for us.

But like I said, Johnny was never satisfied just staying between the ditches. He was always looking for a bigger edge, and if he needed to step a little *over the line*, so be it. It was this bad habit that almost got us whacked one night.

We'd been operating our mini casino and card room for a few months and had settled into a groove, a rhythm. Johnny didn't have a piece of the club, but he got a decent salary and was the de facto manager. He did a good job of keeping his finger on the pulse of the operation, and sometimes when a poker dealer didn't show, or maybe just to keep his hand in, Angles would occasionally fill in.

One night, we had an unexpected guest—Mickey Spinello. Mickey epitomized what a mob guy looked like and dressed like. Always dressed to the nines in a two thousand dollar suit, Mickey was a Mafia don, who had known me since I was a baby. He and his wife were friends of my parents and were in my folks' apartment one Sunday afternoon when his low-life five-year-old son Richard, nearly brought about my early demise. As the story goes, the adults were shooting Craps in our living room, while we kids were off doing who knows what elsewhere. At some point the parents noticed that we were too quiet and went looking for us. Sure enough, there I was, being dangled out of a two-story window by my heels. Mickey raced downstairs to catch me, while my dad snuck up on the kid and grabbed me before I was dropped. Mickey always jokingly said that he wasn't sure he would have caught me because it might have messed up his suit.

But he had always treated me like family, and he had even come to my rescue with some very necessary cash when I had experienced a hugely expensive bad beat in a Vegas Hold'em game. He had even refused any interest, which might have been a first for him. When I thanked him, I jokingly said that if other shylocks heard about this, he might get kicked out of their union. He didn't even laugh. He sounded like Yogi Berra when he said, "Sometimes it's not always business."

But this particular night at our club, it had been slow, so I decided I'd sit in as a shill and play until the table filled up. Johnny was dealing and soon a pretty good game developed. But then I heard something that put my heart in my throat. It was that distinctive sound, a swoosh, produced when the second card is pulled out, rubbing between the first and third card. Hopefully it went unnoticed by everyone else in the room. At least, I prayed it was unnoticed, but I knew instantly that Johnny A. was dealing seconds. Johnny A. was cheating by first holding out certain cards and then dealing those winning cards to specific people. And in *our* game!

The realization was like a kick in the stomach. *What* was he *doing?* How could he be so stupid? My heart nearly pounded out of my chest.

I folded my cards and said "Sorry, guys, but we're going to stop the game for a few minutes," I said. "Let's take a break. Drinks are on the house."

Angles gave me a quizzical glance before averting his eyes. Mickey looked at me with a blank stare. There was no hint that he knew anything was up.

"Johnny," I said as pleasantly as I could, "give me a minute, will you?"

"Sure, Chance."

He spread the deck on the felt and clapped his hands together, the method dealers use to show that they haven't palmed or stolen any chips or haven't concealed anything else in their hands such as pins or marking devices.

"Gentleman, please excuse us," I said as we rose from the table. Catcher was giving me a funny look. I signaled for him and Barry, another buddy of mine, to come with us. As I left the table, Mickey caught my eye, but his expression told me nothing.

We went down the stairs and into a basement back room that doubled as my office. My senses became incredibly acute. There was a strong smell of dirty mops, ammonia, and fear. I looked at Johnny. The other guys didn't have any idea what was going on, but they knew it was big trouble.

"What's up, Chance?"

"You tell me, Johnny."

He shook his head. "I don't know what you mean."

"What's the problem?" Barry asked.

I kept my eyes on Johnny. "You didn't see it, Barry? You didn't hear it?"

"What? What are you talking about?"

"Johnny's dealing seconds."

There was a moment of shocked silence. Johnny was nailed and he knew it. "It was just that one hand, Chance," he said. "I shouldn't have tried it. I don't know what I was thinking."

"That wasn't the only hand," I said.

"I swear it was."

"I've been winning all night—ever since I sat in," I said. "You're telling me it was all square? Don't bullshit me!"

"Well, maybe a couple of hands," he waffled, "but not that many, I swear."

Catcher grimaced. "You'd do that, Johnny? You'd do something like that with Mick sitting in the game?" He sighed and shook his head. He knew it was crazy.

I said, "It doesn't matter who was there. We can't have Mick or anybody else thinking they might get scammed when they come here. Otherwise, we're all dead. Dead as in stone-cold dead."

There wasn't much else to say. Johnny nodded slightly. We stood there for a few seconds, stunned by the magnitude of what had just happened.

Johnny looked at me. "What are you going to do, Chance?"

"Hold him down, Catcher," I said. For a brief, panicked moment, I thought I was going to burst into tears. Johnny A. had been my wingman since we were kids.

Catcher sighed again. "You want me to do it?"

Johnny's eyes were wide with terror.

"No," I said. "No, Catcher. It's got to be me. You know that."

Catcher shrugged and moved toward Johnny. Johnny backpedaled but had nowhere to go. "What're you doing, Chance? I swear it was only a few hands. It wasn't as bad as you think. Listen, I've been kind of out-of-it today. I don't know what got into me. I can make it good."

'That's what we're doing right now," I said. "We can't ever make it right, but we can stop the cancer."

I nodded at Catcher and Barry, and they held him down. He was fighting them, squirming like a trapped animal.

Writhing in panic, he screeched, "Let me go, Chance! You don't have to do this!"

Catcher stretched out Johnny's left arm first, and I broke his thumb with a sharp upward jerk of my wrist. Johnny A. screamed in agony. Then Catcher held out his right arm, and I broke that thumb too.

The crack of broken bones. Johnny's agonized screams. The look on my best friend's face. I felt like throwing up.

Luckily for Johnny, he fainted. Barry and Catcher held him up.

I felt disgusted with myself. With Johnny. With all of us.

"Get him to a doctor," I said. "Then make sure he gets home."

Catcher nodded sadly, and I watched them as they carried Johnny A. up the basement steps, out the rear door, and into the dark.

I went back to the game. Mickey and the others were waiting around the table. I sat down, took all my winnings from the night, and slid them back into the center.

"Take what's yours, Mickey," I said. "And the rest of you. Carve it up. It's all yours. We've had an administrative problem. It's fixed, but we're finished for the night."

One of the other players shrugged and starting picking up chips. "What's going on?" he asked. I said nothing. Then the others started taking back their money too. Mickey stood up with about a grand in chips and walked toward the bar, handing off his chips to one of his guys. I went behind and poured us both a drink.

"Mickey, I'm sorry to say I caught Johnny cheating. I dealt with the situation myself. Catcher and Barry took him to the hospital. He's through here. He won't be dealing any more. Here or anywhere," I said.

Mickey nodded. He didn't seem to have much to add.

"Mick," I said, "I want a favor. I need a favor. I'd like it to end here."

Mickey nodded, again without comment.

"I'm asking you to not do anything. Not to whack him. Not even to bust him up," I said. "No matter what he has done, he was my friend."

Mickey sighed that heavy sigh of his. "I knew what he was doing, Chance."

I was shocked. "You knew? When?"

"Pretty early. I let it go for a while to see how it would play out…"

His guy ambled over and handed him his cash. Mickey slipped it into his jacket pocket. I walked him to the door.

"I'm glad you weren't in on it, Chance."

"I appreciate it, Mick."

"The only thing that surprised me was that you didn't spot it sooner," he said. "You know, it probably wasn't the first time he cheated."

I nodded. "Maybe. I should've been paying closer attention. And thanks, Mickey. I hope we'll keep this to ourselves."

"No other way, man. No other way."

His rueful remark had said it all. I knew that if I hadn't taken care of the situation the way I did when I did, Johnny would have been in a world of hurt and probably planted six feet under. And friend or no friend, maybe I would have been, too.

Chapter Ten

Forgiveness won't change the past, but it might change the future.
—Father Anthony

"So, Chance, Johnny wants the opportunity to set things straight," Norm said. "And I think he's sincere. He wants to sit down with you and say he's sorry. He's got a powerful advocate as well. Father Anthony would like to visit you and Debbie and catch up. I'm sure he also wants to tell you that he thinks everybody deserves a second chance. He'll make a powerful pitch."

And so it happened. Father Anthony leaned on Debbie, and once she was on board, it was just a matter of time for the dominos to fall. I could only hold out for so long, and after all, Johnny A. and I went way back. So I tried to be the *bigger man*, like Debbie wanted. Did I have reservations? I shouldn't have. So why did I have this nervous feeling in my stomach?

I had been blessed to have an incredible mentor during my formative years. Danny Adams was Debbie's stepfather, and I had met him when I was still in high school. He was the guy we kids looked up to and wanted to emulate. He was the guy from the neighborhood who dressed the best, drove a Lincoln, and never had a nine-to-five job. He was a gambler with movie-star good looks, and being a devout church attendee, he was the neighborhood success story—even our parents thought he was a pretty good guy.

Once, while caddying for him, I had noticed that one of his opponents had cheated him. When there was a lull in the action, I told him so in conspiratorial fashion. He never forgot me after that and, subsequently, arranged for me to work for him first as his regular caddy and then as his gambling partner, traveling around southern Ontario and northern New York State. Over the years, we played cards, golf, and gambled on any game where we thought the odds were in our favor. We had a good thing going. I was learning a lot about gambling and, more importantly, about life, and with Danny's tutelage, patience, and bank roll, we were very successful.

However, tragically, one night in Buffalo, while playing poker, Danny and I realized we were being cheated. Initially there was a confrontation, and then words escalated, and Danny was shot. Murdered. I was devastated. It took months, if not years, for me to get at least partially over the incident. But even though it has been years now, I've never forgotten many of the lessons he taught me. And while he is no longer with us, so very often his wise and profound words replay in my head. It happened again in this instance: *"There's no decision tool more powerful than visceral analysis."* I could almost hear him saying that. So why was I ignoring these alarm bells? Maybe it's the moth-to-a-flame syndrome. Or maybe I didn't want to disappoint Debbie. Or maybe it was just because I'm an idiot.

Johnny entered my office somewhat timidly. When we shook hands, I noticed that his right thumb was a little off kilter, as if it hadn't healed quite right. I felt just a twinge of guilt about that but quickly shook it off.

Making small talk to help us get on the same page, I asked him what had been going on in his life. The jungle drums had told me a little, but I sure as hell wasn't prepared for the incredible journey he'd been on. We spent an hour or so just shooting the breeze in my office, and I was hugely impressed. I shouldn't have been; after all, I'd been in the trenches with Johnny for many years and knew firsthand how capable he was. But the multitude of things that he had been involved with over the years just blew me away. He downplayed some of his exploits, like the network of telephone sex providers, and the sports information hotlines, but what really astonished me was his technical expertise and computer-related business acumen.

Johnny had always been tech savvy. As a kid, he was always the first to figure out anything new related to computers or the Internet. He became a walking, talking, freaking genius when it came to computer programming. If he couldn't figure something out of his own accord, he was so brilliant and had so many contacts that he could talk with other programmers on their level and in their own language to get an answer. As a result, he could knit together enough talent to create any new program that he might conceive.

But, again, Johnny couldn't just walk the straight and narrow. He took all that talent and brilliance, and instead of building a new Yahoo or Facebook, he devised a method to skirt the law. He knew that there were many individuals who wanted the capacity of computers, but they also needed to be sure that if their computers fell into the wrong hands, the content would disappear. Not just corrupted or compromised—the info had to become fumes. So he created a fail-safe method that would actually burn a computer's hard drive into oblivion. His method required the operator to perform a certain ritual when starting their computer—otherwise, the hard drive would vaporize.

The technology Johnny developed wasn't unlike the audio and video devices seen in *Mission Impossible*, which self-destructed after a one-time message was played. Johnny's technical savvy allowed him to program the computer in such a way that after three attempts using the wrong password, the computer's hard drive would go blank.

He accomplished this by wiring a unique high-voltage capacitor that he had designed, onto the motherboard attached to the hard drive, and on the third attempt using the wrong password, a high-voltage electrical surge would vaporize all the data storage and completely melt the hard drive to a puddle of plastic. He also took the security aspect one step further by incorporating into his device the ability to activate this feature wirelessly. It could be done from anywhere using a cell phone. That was Johnny—one step ahead. Even the forensic techies at Homeland Security marveled at his fail-safe innovation.

Then, to market this highly toxic technology, he went to his roots. Did he go to Wall Street or Bay Street to do a stock offering? Did he go to the retail market? No, Johnny had to go the dark route. Taking a page out of the Dell promotion manual, he geared his advertising to a specific user market: the gambling community. There were bookies in every part of the country who needed to record their transactions but who wanted the assurance that if their computer fell into the wrong hands, all the data would go to information heaven. And it did just that. A Nano second before the hard drive became toast, all the info was uplifted and bounced to a secure site in a foreign jurisdiction that not even Johnny could access. It would take the combined knowledge of several individuals around the world to provide the sequencing key to unlock the info.

Word had gotten around about his stupid cheating attempt, and ostracized, he moved to the West Coast. Unable to deal cards, he set up a Dial 900 sports information hot line. He went to all the cities where there was an NHL hockey team and befriended or otherwise made a deal with a sports writer, broadcaster, trainer, or really anybody close to the team. For a C-note a week, they tipped him off to anything unusual: big star gets pissed, wife walks out, goalie stubs toe; whatever. If it had the potential to affect the outcome of the game, Johnny A. got to know about it first.

He started out charging two dollars a minute for customers who wanted team updates or his recommended picks, but he soon realized that the bigger bucks were to be made betting the Canadian government's Sports Select wagering tickets. By piecing off sport team trainers for inside information on injuries and other internal team problems, he made a ton betting parlays—all tax-free. In Canada gambling winnings are not taxable. But Johnny was so successful, and made so much money, that the Canada Revenue Agency tried to tax his winnings. They took him to court, but he even beat them.

But Johnny just could not stop being Johnny. Always a little kinky, he hired a team of stay-at-home moms and out-of-work guys and set up phone porn lines. He was constantly innovating. He was the first to set up phone porn lines geared to the gay community. Within two years it was as if he was printing money.

Eventually, he did have a bit of a setback. His porn business relied heavily on advertising and he had initially relied on print media. But when the Internet came into its own, he saw the potential, and soon his ads completely dominated the space. However, in America, success spawns imitators, and his sites soon had legions of competitors.

But brilliant Johnny trumped them once again. Because he was one of the early users of Internet advertising, he understood every nuance. He had developed his search engines in conjunction with Google and Yahoo and understood that it was strictly a numbers game. For every hundred hits, 40 percent would find his initial messages provocative enough to click through to registration, and about 15 percent of those would sign up and spend an average of about seventy-five dollars per month religiously. However, his success was soon a beacon for imitators, and eventually his business began to drop off. It had been great during the early stages, and being the only game in town, his conversion rate was high. For every buck he spent on advertising, he'd get a $1.50 return.

But the new competition kept eroding his piece of the pie, so he decided he had to eliminate or otherwise hurt these troublemakers. He had been paying the search engines about six dollars for each of his registrants and had opted to pay another two dollars to dominate at the top of the page. His cost each month was in the tens of thousands, and he knew his competitors were paying at least as much, if not more. So he moved his site down to the bottom of the preferences and from time to time even took it offline entirely. At the same time he set up a series of IP addresses registered around the world, and his renegade sites began to kidnap the hits that had been going to his competitor's sites. An interested customer would click on a site, and his click would be seamlessly and instantly routed to one of Johnny's new IP addresses, where it would languish and then dissolve. Unfortunately for the customer, their hard-on would be long gone because they'd never get a call back from a talk partner. But because of Johnny's strategy, his competition would still have to pay the six dollars for the click but would receive no corresponding revenue from the user.

It only took a month or so for his competition to feel the pressure and to see the light. After a decent interval, Johnny would visit and help them understand that they might want to buy him out, or maybe even give him an override. Of course, the quid pro quo was that he would allow their sites to again function as normal. He made another fortune. Once again, those broken thumbs were the best thing that ever happened to him.

So Johnny was back in the fold. But he wasn't the same old Johnny. Actually, that wasn't true. He was absolutely the same: only different. I sometimes caught him watching me...maybe even glaring at me. If he saw that I'd noticed, he'd immediately grin and say something goofy to get a quick laugh. But I was starting to think he hadn't forgotten. And even though he had deserved it, and even though it might have saved his life, I was starting to think that maybe he still carried a grudge. Maybe he always would.

But we could get past it, right?

We began to function with old animosities and prior conflicts hopefully mended. And very quickly we were blowing and going like never before. All too soon, Father Anthony had to return to Toronto, but Johnny and Country stayed in Balboa and quickly found new ways to make a buck.

Country found an entrepreneurial side that he didn't know existed. He began importing golf-club components from China. The knock-offs were great for everyone except the original manufacturer. He incorporated up-to-date design and technology, and except for a minor name change, his clubs were virtually identical to the original. Country had the components shipped to San Vida, where the heads and grips were installed on the shafts, and he was soon having them shipped to enthusiastic buyers all over America. And best of all, by having the clubs assembled locally, the 1,000 percent profit was retained tax-free in Balboa.

Country was funny, though. He'd never had any real money before, so he didn't know how to act once it started pouring in. It was as if he couldn't believe his good fortune would last. We used to kid him that he was as tight as bark to a tree. But our wisecracks didn't bother him a bit. He said, "I've got it and I'm keeping it. If I need something, and it flies, floats, or fucks, I can rent it." We all thought he was taking it a bit too far, and all his wife, Jackie, would say is "See what I've had to put up with all these years? He's a wacko. He never does anything I suggest, except once. I suggested that he get a penis enlarger. He did. She's twenty-two. Her name's Mona."

She was as bad as Country.

Chapter Eleven

Nobody's always a boy scout. Not even a boy scout.
—Frank Underwood, House of Cards

While waiting for the deep thinkers of the government, the port authority, and Diamond Resorts to get their act together, I had other things to do, including interviewing appraisal firms and meeting the headhunters who would help me build our resort-management team. I was, however, determined not to let the process become all-consuming.

In addition to spending quality time with Debbie and our beautiful daughter, Rylee, on the weekends, I made sure that I got home each night at six for dinner. That gave our little family an opportunity to chat about the events of the day and share our plans for the days and weeks ahead. Debbie was totally immersed with her involvement with the Mary Star of the Sea School, and I took enormous pride in her contribution to the school, the church, and in local affairs. I told her that it was too bad she wasn't Balboan because she was becoming so popular she could have run for office.

So we were like Modern Family. Everything was coming up roses. All this domesticity and corporate responsibility, however, needed to be balanced with a modicum of athletic endeavor, which, again, usually meant a little golf.

There was a bit of lull in the action one bright sunny day, so I hooked up with my usual companion, Dougie T. (known to one and all as "Solinski"—go figure), for a quick eighteen. After hitting the customary zillion practice balls and two practice putts, we headed for the first tee where we were joined by a walk-on. He said he was a lawyer from Miami over for a few days of R&R. He seemed like a cool guy, and being a lawyer, we quickly nicknamed him "Loop Hole." Because we were a threesome playing behind foursomes, we had a lot of time to visit, and as I always look to spice up the festivities, by the fourth hole I had a pretty good idea of how I could ensnare him into a proposition bet.

By the eighth hole, the stage was set. We had talked about sports and gambling, and his vibe was that he was a bit of a player, so it didn't take much promotion to interest him in a bet. Waiting for the group ahead to clear the green, I took my eight iron and wandered over to a spot about twenty feet behind a group of three towering palm trees, which were about 120 yards from the green. As I simulated my swing, I said, "You know, I think I can hit my ball over these trees and onto the green."

"Impossible," he said. "If you hit it high enough to get it over the tree, your trajectory will only allow the ball to go forward about forty or fifty yards."

"Yeah," I said, "but there's a gap in the palm fronds about the size of a basketball, and maybe I can do it if you give me a couple of shots."

He must have thought I was crazy, but he agreed to a bet of $100.

I confirmed the bet. "I'll hit the ball over or through the palms to or onto the green." And I would get two shots. He was salivating. So I wandered back over and had him agree to the spot. I then got over the ball as if to hit it. But I stopped and went around to the other side of the ball, intending to hit it *away* from the trees to a spot that would be just far enough away that I could safely hit my second shot over the trees and onto the green. But I started laughing so hard at the expression on his face when he realized my plan that I hit the ball too hard, and it went forty-five yards, over a cart path, and ended up in a swale and a downhill lie. From there it was an impossible shot, so I paid up the hundred, but we had a hell of a laugh.

It took me a few holes to recover from my faux pas, but never being one to let an opportunity go unexploited, I soon had a new plan designed to turn my lemon into lemonade. I took their razzing for another few holes, but when there was another lull in the action, I proposed another bet. It was a perfect setup. The pump was primed. The hook was set. Loop Hole was engaged. This time I'd take no prisoners.

We were on a par-4, 364-yard hole, slightly uphill to a rear pin. I told him that if he would give me one stroke, I would play the entire hole backward.

He was skeptical.

I said, "For twice the amount we played for on the last bet. All you have to do is beat me. If you win you win. If you don't beat me, you lose. It is a simple win or lose bet."

He hit a 280-yard screamer right down the middle. Even Solinski was impressed. Loop Hole was pleased with himself. His smile waned a bit, however, when using a backward stance, I cracked a 230-yard drive down the middle of the fairway. Unfortunately, my drive ended up on the downhill slope of a small ridge, giving me a lot tougher shot than I would have liked. This appeared to make Loop Hole happy, which I didn't think was very nice.

But even a blind squirrel finds an acorn from time to time. I hit a career soft draw to about fifteen feet from the pin. I was sure I could hear his sphincter muscle slam shut. But there was no quit in Loop Hole, and he hit a short wedge to about ten feet.

This is when it got really good. As we approached the green, he said something like, "Well, if I can make this putt, and you miss, at least I can eke out a tie."

I could hardly contain myself and keep from laughing as I reminded him of the bet, "I hate to break it to you, but remember the bet—win or lose. You have to beat me to win. Otherwise, you lose."

He almost fell down laughing when he reviewed the bet in his head. He wasn't even chagrined when he admitted out loud, "I heard it. I remember it. I just didn't put two and two together." He was a great sport, even when I putted my ball backward to about two inches from the hole for a tap-in par.

When the match was over, Solinski begged off our invitation for drinks and said his good-byes, and Loop Hole and I adjourned to the clubhouse, where he learned that this was not your typical country club. I bought a few drinks at the bar, putting a big dent in the C-note I had won. We then retired to the men's locker room, where we found several Gin games in progress. Loop Hole was a keener and suggested he'd like to play.

I said, "Buddy, I'm all for playing Gin, sometime. But if you're all fired up about playing cards, why don't we have dinner first. The reason there are so many Gin players is because a poker game is scheduled to start about 8:00 PM. When we finish dinner, if you're still so inclined, we can decide then if we want to play.

Loophole agreed and during dinner, and with thanks to a few more glasses of wine, I took the opportunity to share some background about the game and who we might find playing.

As I ran through the list I found that even I was amazed at the cast of characters that had found their way to this Caribbean island. I gave Loophole a somewhat sanitized description of some of the main characters but I couldn't help but elaborate about *top cop* Greg Goodkey.

I said, "There's another guy who you might have noticed as we wandered through the men's locker room. Big white guy about 45 years old. Did you see him?"

"No, not really. But we were only in there for a few minutes and there was a lot going on."

"Well he's a bit of a local hero, a legend, whatever. He's Greg Goodkey. Balboan, born and raised. But after high school he went off to Virginia to study law enforcement. After completing his schooling he came back to work in his family's furniture business, eventually he becoming the company's president. He went on to expand the business throughout the Caribbean, and did very well for himself when an English conglomerate bought into the companies. He's a very capable guy and is still on their board, but he's no longer active on an operational basis. All of which gives him more time to follow his passion, which is police work.

"When he returned to Balboa after graduating he joined the police force as a trainee cadet on a part time basis. So while he was moving up through the corporate world, he was doing the same thing in law enforcement. Eventually he became the head of the Balboan Police Marine Patrol, and he's still doing that today.

"And by the way, if you ever want to talk about strange bedfellows. In one of those Gin games you witnessed there was both the former head of a large drug cartel who used to, or to some extent still uses Balboa as a transshipping point for illegal drugs into the USA. And at the same table was the head of the police department who is charged with the task of taking him down. But that's only a sidebar to my story. As I said Greg is a bit of a local legend because of a couple of things. One of which happened right here at the club.

"There had been the usual Thursday-night poker game and Greg had taken it on the chin pretty hard. Lost about fifteen thousand dollars. And because he had only taken five grand to the game, he had to go to the bank in the morning giving him little time to get to the course for his nine-twenty tee time. He was playing with three of the guys from the poker game from the night before, and because he was so late arriving they had already hit their drives and were halfway down the fairway by the time he got there giving him no opportunity to pay them the money he owed them. Incidentally, that group typically plays five-hundred dollar Nassau and fifty dollars a hole, so with presses, a lot of coin can change hands. As a result, most of them carry a lot of cash.

"Do you remember the second hole? Long par five dogleg around the corner to the right? Well, no sooner had they began to putt, when a couple of masked dudes came out of the bushes, guns drawn, and held them up. It must have been a pretty scary scene.

"But this is where it gets interesting, According to his playing partners, when the robbers approached Greg, he didn't say or do anything for a moment. He just stood there, looking at them and taking it all in. The bad guys quickly herded everyone to their golf bags and forced them to hand over their cash, wallets and jewelry. But while Greg had gone reluctantly over to his cart, he hadn't made a move to hand over his valuables. The one robber, who the other referred to as "Tree," finally stuck his shotgun in Greg's stomach and told him to hand over his cash or he'd blast him apart. Finally Greg, who still hadn't said anything the entire time, said, 'OK, you've got me. You've got a gun on me and there isn't anything I can do. But just give me a second, and I won't cause you any trouble.' And with that, Greg pulled his bank roll out of his golf bag and turned to his golf partners and said, 'Ok Sy, I lost four thousand to you last night. Here it is.' Then he went to the next guy and paid him the thirty-five hundred he had just lost to him and said, 'Now you're paid.' And to the last guy he said, 'Here's your three thousand two hundred dollars. Now all of you guys are paid from the game last night.' And with that he handed over the balance of his cash to the dumfounded thieves.

"And of course the thieves quickly regained their composure and promptly grabbed his remaining cash. Then turned to his now protesting -playing partners who had just been paid, and took that cash off them as well. Let me tell you, those guys were double pissed. There was considerable gnashing of teeth when the robbers disappeared back into the bush, but as far as Greg was concerned he had paid all his poker debts. Now *that's* what I call guts!!! He's one cool dude. It's no wonder he's a bit of a local icon."

"Jeezz!! What an incredible story. Talk about balls." And just as his last syllable died away there was Debbie with her usual impeccable timing sliding into a seat saying." If I had two I'd be king!."

Loop Hole choked on his drink.

"Debbie my sweetheart, meet my new, almost best friend Loop Hole. Lawyer extraordinaire from Miami. Loop Hole this is my wife Debbie," I said as I leaned over and gave her a quick kiss.

It took my new lawyer friend a moment or two to regain his composure, but after we ordered Debbie a glass of wine and exchanged some brief niceties, I relaunched into my story about Greg.

"What I'm about to tell you is only a rumor and I wouldn't want it to get spread around because of me. As you've probably surmised this is a little bit like the *Old West* out here in the islands. Few questions are asked and even fewer are answered. And to start with you really should see Greg's computer screen saver. I don't know how many images are on it but I'd guess it would be somewhere in the low hundreds."

"Images of what?"

"Bodies. One of the most shocking experiences of my life was when Greg showed me the screen. I was sitting beside him at his desk when all of a sudden I noticed his eyes well up and tears began rolling down his cheeks. Frankly I wasn't prepared for this big two-hundred pound, six-foot-two cop to sit beside me and cry."

"Jesus…" muttered Loop Hole, obviously surprised.

"Yeah, it was pretty remarkable. We had been talking about the 'go-slow boats' and the 'go fast boats', and how they were used to transport drugs to the Balboan and Bahamian Islands in preparation for being trans-shipped into the U S main land. Greg had been relating how the go-slow boats would sail up from Haiti or Jamaica with a load of weed or cocaine and dump overboard the waterproofed cargo or bales upwind or up-current from their intended destination. The prevailing wind or current would then cause the "square groupers" as they're called locally, to wash up close to shore. The cargo would then be dragged up and across the beaches and hidden in the trees, waiting for the go-fast boats to pick them up when the timing was right. Those go-fast boats scoot like a bat-out-of-hell and can jet across the gulf-stream in less than an hour.

The key though is the go-slow boats. They never attract any attention primarily because they're not in American waters and over here in the "out islands" it's a case of 'who cares.' Drug running has gone on for years.

"But Greg went on to tell me that there's a new smuggling venture. It's the same drill but a different cargo. Instead of booze or drugs it's now humans. Greg said the bad guys charge six thousand dollars per person. It's the same MO as with the weed, and he and his marine patrol were responsible for arresting many smugglers and confiscating their boats. He said he would arrest them and return the boats to their rightful owners whenever possible---in other words if the owners were still alive, and turn the smugglers over to the U S authorities in Miami. But it only took about ninety days for the perps to go through the U S legal system and be deported back to Balboa and the Bahamas.

"Greg said he played that revolving door game for quite a while, but then he learned that the Florida police were beginning to find drowned bodies washed up on the beaches. Evidently the creeps were picking the up the hopeful immigrants over in the islands and racing across the Gulf Stream until the boat got three or four hundred yards offshore. Then they would tell everyone to get out. They would force them overboard regardless of whether or not the passengers could swim. The greedy and heartless smugglers didn't want to take a chance of running their boats onto shore because that would increase their chances of getting caught while their passengers disembarked.

"Greg has a really hard edge that not everybody gets to see. But just between us, he started *running them*. That's a not-so-nice way of saying that when he and his crew caught smugglers in the open sea, he would transfer those being smuggled onto his cutter and then disable the engine of the bad guy's boat, letting the smugglers drift away in the Gulf Stream… next stop England. One might even speculate that from time to time his cutter might have an accident…. aka a collision with the smugglers' boats: running up their transom and thus causing the boat to sink with the perps still aboard. Harsh, yes. Cruel? I'm not so sure. Either way it was effective. And if you're wondering if it's all true, and you're looking for clues, the name of his boat is *"Pragmatic."*

"Jesus Christ Chance! I see what you mean---- this really is like the Old West."

I guess I got on a bit of a roll and prompted by dutiful wife Debbie, who had heard them all before, I gave Loop Hole a run down on some of the characters he might be facing if we decided to play poker.

At some point, along about my fifth story, Loop Hole commented on the number of guys who had been adorned with nick names. This caused me to pause, take a breath and reflect on his observation. He was right. Almost every guy had a rather colorful moniker. I had mentioned: Gold Finger our local gynecologist, Hackin Drac… his running mate who did plastic surgery and also provided clean blood transfusions and new blood replacements for those who needed to show the courts that they were "now clean". AKA Keith Richards, after his Toronto drug bust. My buddies Angles (who always had one) and Catcher (who looked like one). And Wall Street Wally a stock promoter from Vancouver. Also Moonie. His real name is Neil Armstrong, like the first man on the moon, Neil liked the name association. In fact he even signed his checks and chits with… *Moonie.*

Loop Hole got into the nick name thing and we had a lot of fun relating the nick names to the individuals. Finally I capped off the evening when I challenged both Loop Hole and Debbie to figure out why we called one guy Buster. Wine induced they came up with a ton of guesses. All wrong. I said "Ok, follow the bouncing ball. We call him Buster which is a derivative of his *full nick name* which is Busted. Get it???" Blank quizzical looks all around. *"Busted* as in *Busted Flat."* Still no hint of understanding. And of course by now I'm laughing and enjoying their confusion. "Ok. One last clue. His real name is Robert McGee." I let it hang there. And hang there. Finally I couldn't contain myself anymore. Laughing I said, " His name is BOBBY. Bobby MCGEE!!! As in *Busted Flat* in Baton Rouge… Waitin for a train." Laughter all around and a great way to end a perfect evening.

The next day wasn't so perfect.

Chapter Twelve

That minister was so dumb
it would take him two hours to watch Sixty Minutes.
—Chance Daly, Balboa

As soon as I got the call from Paul Bethel, I knew something was off kilter. I could just sense it. He asked if I could come to Playas to meet his minister. His comments were rather oblique, and when a guy you have known for years suddenly goes all formal on you, you know something's in the wind. In this case, I knew the odds were that it wasn't going to be good.

The meeting was scheduled for the next day, and because I happened to know that Greg was flying down to Playas in the morning, I called to see if Norm and I could catch a ride in his new twin-engine Cessna. The trip turned out to be pretty cool. Although the plane only holds eight passengers, it still requires both a pilot and copilot. And because it's such a short hop from San Vida to Playas, there isn't much for the copilot to do. Just to make conversation, I asked him what his role was.

He said, "I am the captain's sexual adviser."

Of course, I was immediately thinking that the copilot should be called the *procurement officer* because he was probably in charge of finding girls for the pilot when they were in a new town, but no.

"What the hell is a *sexual adviser?*" I asked.

"The captain told me that when he wants any *fucking advice* from me, he'll ask for it."

Once we landed, it was only forty-five minutes before we were whisked into the ante room of Government House on Bay Street. We would have been even earlier had we not stopped to pick up a couple of people on the way. But even with that small detour, we were still ten minutes early for our scheduled appointment, which we thought was only going to be with Minister of Tourism and my old buddy, Deputy Minister Paul Bethel. Our trip from San Vida had gone very smoothly, and we thought it might be a good omen of things to come. But an hour later, we weren't so sure.

A number of well-dressed gentlemen had presented themselves to the receptionist, and they all had been quickly directed in ahead of us. Finally, an hour and twenty minutes after the appointed time, Paul came out, apologizing profusely, and ushered us into a large room, which contained what looked like the largest boardroom table on the planet. Obviously this hallowed hall was used for caucus sessions, as the massive table could easily seat forty people. It was almost a third full. Norm and I took our seats at one end, and they quickly got down to introductions. In addition to the minister and Paul, there was a deputy minister from the prime minister's office and the two Bay Street lawyers on the government side. Mr. Goldberg, the Diamond Resort CFO, and the regional vice president of Diamond Resorts were also there, along with a couple of lawyers from Wall Street. Heavy firepower indeed!

"Gentlemen," the minister began, "we have both a problem and an opportunity. Mr. Daly, as a result of your due diligence and efforts, not only have *we* become increasingly aware of the dormant value of the King's Inn Resort, but the Grand Balboan

Port Authority, who holds us all hostage as a result of their licensing agreement, has begun to show more interest as well. To bring you up to date, this project has created strange bedfellows. Initially deputy minister Bethel gave you free rein, unfettered encouragement, and total access to the resort. This was done even though the resort was, and remains, owned by Diamond Resorts. A complicated situation to be sure. And now the Port Authority has reentered the fray, further complicating matters. Fortunately, all parties have finally come together in a spirit of cooperation and mutual respect, and there is every likelihood that the King's Own Resort shall, like a phoenix, rise once again to its position of preeminence in the Caribbean."

Good grief, I thought. *Is this guy kidding or what? Just say what's on your damn mind, and quit this soapbox nonsense!*

"Thank you, Mr. Minister," Goldberg chimed in. "And that's an excellent way to start and finish these discussions. Mr. Daly, the government of Balboa and Diamond Resorts, ably supported by the Port Authority, has created a triumvirate joint venture with the intention of owning and operating the King's Own Resort."

"And where does that leave us?" I asked.

"We would like to negotiate some settlement and reward and thank you for all your hard work," said the minister.

"I'm disappointed to lose the opportunity to buy the property, but the million-dollar break fee will go a long way toward assuaging my hurt feelings."

"That's where we have a bit of an issue," said Paul. "Everyone from the ministerial level, right up to the prime minister himself, is adamantly opposed to paying you one million for what they consider to be only three months' work. There must be some sort of middle ground."

I remained calm, although I sure didn't feel it as I began. "Gentlemen, let's be clear. I know that the government has already approved paying me the million. They did that from the get-go when they approved and entered into our sales contract. In addition, we have, as I'm sure your lawyers have conveyed, an ironclad option to buy the resort. And until just minutes ago, it was our intention to announce our commitment to do so. If fact, we intended to make the announcement *today*."

"But Mr. Daly, up until now, you have been silent on the entire purchase side of the process. And you expect us to believe that you were just about to announce your intention to buy the property? We are more than prepared to be fair, but paying you a million dollars is impossible. Our board and the government won't stand for it."

"Do you think I'm posturing?" I asked. "Did you see those two people who accompanied us here? They are waiting in your reception area for us. We picked them up on our way here from the airport. One is Shannon Tannas, a photographer. And Mr. Minister, you must know the other one—Bruce Klippenstein, the editor of the *Playas Guardian* newspaper. They are here to do a story on our announcement that we are buying the King's Own Resort."

It got real quiet real fast.

"May we caucus?" asked Goldberg.

"By all means. Norm and I will get a coffee and will be back in ten minutes. When we come back, all we want is for you to say yes or no. And if it's yes, then I've got some ideas about how we can work together on the optics to make our fees more palatable. If it's no…well, it may take a while, but I'll get my money one way or the other."

A few minutes later over coffee, Norm asked, "Chance, are you telling me you were going to announce that we were removing conditions and that we were buying the King's Own Resort?"

"Quite the contrary. I got into thinking about the tone of Paul's phone call to me and realized these buggers were going to have us "walk the plank." They were going to turf us after all our hard work and probably try to pay us a fraction of what they really owed us. I thought that by having the press here it would serve to keep the smoke out of the system and the bullshit to a minimum."

Ten minutes later, we were back in the boardroom, and the minister announced, "Gentlemen, the Commonwealth of Balboa always pays its bills, and as such, we are pleased to have benefited to such an extent from the technical expertise of Mr. Chance Daly and his team of experts. Your check for one million dollars is being prepared as we speak. Now, Mr. Daly, you said you had some ideas for us?"

"Yes, sir, I do," I said as a palpable sense of relief washed over me, which I hoped wasn't too obvious to the assembled group. "But first let's deal with the media. We've kept them cooling their heels too long, and I'd like to give them a story."

After the all-too-loquacious minister met the media folks to make the announcement that the King's Own Resort and Casino was going to be reopened with thirteen hundred jobs for San Vida residents, we got down to sharing our thoughts on how to best bring this wonderful facility back into service.

"Gentlemen, there is a role for everyone at this table," I said back in the boardroom. "First and foremost, it will be imperative for the government to fully support every initiative taken by the managers of the property, including the training and the deployment of personnel. Ownership must be seen as a combined effort, and all parties must convey a unified front. The first step must be to quickly appoint a general manager who will be both the public face and the lightning rod for all the heat that is going to rain down on the project. He or she should be responsible to the owner's board of directors, but subject to their unanimous directives, the manager must have clear and unfettered control of the resort."

"Why is this so important that it needs to be discussed at this early stage?"

"Because the success of the resort and the success of your partnership will all depend on attitude. And that starts at the top. I can assure you that Diamond Resorts is capable of doing a wonderful job with the management of both the hotel and the golf course. But they are not miracle workers. The staff who operate the hotel must recognize that it is their attitude that is of paramount importance in helping guests enjoy their stay. Therefore, if any staff cannot wear a smile while carrying out his or her duties, then they have no business being in the hospitality industry and should be encouraged to find employment elsewhere. It's as simple as that. And not to put too fine a point on it, but employees must fully understand that they will have no back-door recourse to a relative in government in the event they are being disciplined or fired. There can be only one boss, and that has to be the resort GM, and every stakeholder must give him or her their full support."

This was kind of a *"come to Jesus"* wake-up call for all assembled. But much to their credit, everybody, including those from government, agreed on the need for all to embrace, and to consistently deliver, this message.

So being on a bit of a roll, I continued, "No disrespect, Mr. Goldberg, but if I may, my team of analysts also concluded that while Diamond Resorts does a marvelous job of running the hospitality side of your business, they do a correspondingly awful job of managing casinos. As a result, there is a good chance that the operation of the casino will have a negative impact on the performance of this resort. Therefore, we would recommend that you either fix the problem at source or close the casino completely."

There was a pregnant silence.

"What? What do you mean?" asked Goldberg, clearly taken by surprise.

"Mr. Goldberg, this is an issue that can't be done justice in one or two sentences, and I sure don't want to come across as being too critical or as being a smart-ass."

"Please go ahead," requested the minister. "You certainly have my attention."

"Well then, if everybody is OK with it, please allow me to elaborate. After all, you are paying us a million dollars as a break fee, so in consideration, we are pleased to share with you some of what we have learned.

"First, I am proud of what our team has accomplished. We spent considerable time, effort, and money analyzing the property and the status of operations, right up to the point in time when the hurricanes hit. With the benefit of being able to look back *via the rearview mirror*, we took the opportunity to review what you did right, and conversely, because we wanted to learn from your mistakes, we really focused on any aspect that we found, where we thought something might have been done wrong or what might have been done better. That's why we can state unequivocally that Diamond Resorts will do a wonderful job of managing the hotel and golf courses again, as long as the government allows them the same labor consideration in San Vida that they provided in Playas."

"As I said, that won't be a problem," intoned the minister.

"Also, you should either shut down the casino or get somebody to operate it who knows what they are doing."

"Chance, what do you mean?" asked Goldberg as his face began to turn crimson. "We don't have many casinos, but the ones we do have make money."

"But they don't make *much* money, and the profits they generate are often produced to the detriment of the hotels and the hotel guests they serve," I said.

"That just doesn't make any sense to me," blustered Goldberg.

"Or to me. Or me," the group around the board table said in confusion.

"If you don't want to hear what I'm saying, then just say so," I said, raising my hands in a gesture of surrender.

"No, of course we want to hear. But you have to understand that this is hard for us to digest. We've been in the hospitality business for years and have a billion-dollar balance sheet, and you're going to tell us that we don't know what we're doing with an important segment of our business?" I could almost see the steam pouring from Goldberg's ears.

"That's right, and furthermore, with your permission, I'm willing to make two more statements that are guaranteed to annoy everybody at this table. You may even question my sanity." I smiled ruefully.

"You're probably right about that" cracked Paul, relieving a bit of the tension. Fortunately, everyone laughed—at least a little.

I began, "Number one, if left to their own initiatives, the steps Diamond Resorts will want to take to improve the profitability of the casino will not be in the best interests of the Commonwealth of Balboa. Number two, the partners will have different investment and profit philosophies, which will become more apparent as time goes on. They don't realize this right now, but please allow me to explain."

"Chance, this is way over my head," said Goldberg.

"Mine too," said the minister.

"And mine" chorused the others in the room.

"I told you that you weren't going to like it." I smiled. "But indulge me. Let's first all agree that the motivation for the government to become a partner is to help the King's Own Resort get reopened. The Balboan government does not normally invest in hotel operations, but it did so for a number of reasons, not the least of which is their desire to provide thirteen hundred very important jobs for their constituents. Their primary motivation is to restart an operation that will be sustainable and ongoing. They also want to help create an amenity that will bring tourists to their country, and they want to ensure that those tourists will want to keep returning. In a perfect world, they would also want their investment to be profitable, but to the government, that's a bonus. Mostly, they want the King's Own to be an engine of commerce, providing jobs not just for today, but also for decades to come. In other words, they have a long-term perspective."

"And how is that at variance with our goals?" asked Goldberg, somewhat accusingly.

"Diamond Resorts is a public company. As such, the future is now. Not in two or three or ten years. It's *now!* Agreed?" Without waiting for a response, I went on, "Your job and the job of every executive in the company is to make profits this quarter and every quarter."

"Well, sure, Chance, everybody knows that. But we invest for the future as well. We have capital improvement programs and training programs that are ongoing, and they're all geared to enhance profitability for the future," said Goldberg.

"No argument. But I'm referring to the operations of your business. For discussion purposes, let's agree that if a division or an operation could generate more profits immediately, just by turning a dial, would you do it?" I asked.

"Of course. But I say 'of course' theoretically, because I don't know the details or the background," said Goldberg cautiously.

"How about in the casino?"

"Again, of course."

"What about with the slot machines?"

"OK, I can see where you're going. But what's wrong with enhancing the return on the slot machines by adjusting the payouts?" queried Goldberg.

"Nothing in theory, but what if it was done to the detriment of the casino and, ultimately, the Resort?"

Without waiting for a reply, I went on. "Mr. Goldberg, here it is…plain and simple. Every one of your casinos we visited as part of our due diligence process was being robbed blind." I paused at this point, waiting for that extraordinary remark to be fully processed by all present. "And they are being robbed because they are being operated by accountants or hotel executives who possess little or no knowledge of the gaming industry. Now stay with me here. I am stating that because casino profits are too low, because they are being robbed without Diamond Resorts knowing that they are being robbed, that to compensate, their accountant's trained response is to adjust the slot machines to produce a higher return or, in other words, improved profits. An accountant's natural tendency is to adjust the house's hold percentage upward to achieve a higher or more acceptable profit. And that, gentlemen, is Chance Daly's Law of Diminishing Return. If that misguided philosophy is employed here in San Vida, the result will be at variance with the interest of the government." I paused for a minute to let my comments sink in and then continued. "The government wants to have its guests enjoy themselves and have a pleasant, fun time so that they will keep returning. However, we know that tourists will be less likely to return if they've had a negative experience. And they sure as hell will feel they've had a negative experience if they believe they were ripped off when they played in the casino."

"Now hold on," protested Goldberg. "Hold on. You've said a number of things, some of which are way out in left field. Fundamentally, you're saying that because profits are down in the casinos, we are jacking up the take on the machines to an unrealistic percentage, and the players aren't getting enough play for their gambling dollar."

"You nailed it," I said.

"Well, Chance, we all know your reputation. And maybe the slot-machine percentages have been adjusted to a fault, and I can and will check into that. But just what do you mean that our casinos are being robbed?"

"You are being cheated by players, management, and your staff, day in and day out."

"Impossible. At least, I should say, highly unlikely. How could we be? We have the best security systems and the best technology available," protested Goldberg.

"Well, you *are* being robbed, and I can prove it."

There was a chorus of "How? How are you going to do that?"

The bait was offered. The trap was set. And, as usual, all I had needed to do was hook an ego.

Chapter Thirteen

If Chance Daly wants to bet you that an eagle is going to fly in the window and piss in your ear, don't take the bet. But if you do, be sure to wear old clothes and earplugs, because for sure you're going to get an ear full of eagle piss.
—Seymour Harris, Rancho Mirage, California

"Gentlemen, you are paying us a million dollars because we showed you that the value of a wonderful asset, the King's Own Resort, could and should be unlocked. It took a lot of effort, analysis, and professional experience to arrive at our conclusions. There were also considerable third-party costs associated with that due diligence. Those costs totaled $397,000 for architectural and engineering studies, sales and marketing analyses, personnel evaluations, investigative work, and eventually new business operating plans for the hotel, the casino, and the golf courses. All this material would, and can, accrue to the benefit of your business. And, not incidentally, you will have to replicate much of it unless we can come to some sort of an arrangement. We are prepared to turn all this valuable material over to you at our cost. Or you can have it for free. I am stating that your casinos are being cheated, and I can prove it."

"How are you going to prove it?" asked Goldberg.

"I will prove it by playing blackjack in your casino and cheating while being observed by all of you. And if you wish, your security personnel are welcome to attend as well. I realize this is a pretty bold statement. I suggest that the best way to prove my point will be to have a blackjack game set up in the old casino in which I will be the sole player. I'll start with $100,000 in chips, and the casino can start with $100,000, or even $200,000. And the bet will be that I guarantee that I will win all your chips by cheating before you will win mine. I propose that you can stand around the table and observe, and your security people can monitor overhead through the *eyes in the sky* as they would normally do. And if anyone catches me cheating, or if I lose my chips, then you can have all the materials that we have so painstakingly assembled, at no cost. However, if I win all your chips, you will pay me only the $397,000, which is our third-party cost. All the cost for our time and effort expended to date, we'll throw in gratis. "

"You mean to say that you will cheat our blackjack game in our casino while you're being watched? And if we catch you, you will give us $397,000 worth of studies and reports for no cost?" asked Goldberg incredulously. "Impossible! Can you give us a few minutes while we discuss your proposition?"

"Of course."

As expected, it all came together as I had hoped. It was agreed that we would reconvene in one week at the casino that had been shut down since the hurricanes hit and the resort had been closed. In the meantime, we would ensure that the interior would be cleaned, made game-ready, and a dealer hired. Goldberg would bring their own cards to make sure I wasn't using marked decks. They would also have their own security personnel scrutinize the action. All I would have to do was bring the knowledge, the talent, and just a touch of larceny.

A week later, at 2:00 p.m., it was Showtime. Lights, Camera, Action! Security was watching me like starving hawks. I began by saying, "Gentlemen, there are a hundred ways or more to cheat at blackjack, and I'm not including card counting, which is more a science than cheating. What you are about to witness is only one."

"Are we ready? And your name is?" I asked the dealer.

"I'm Jim Clayton."

"Guys, this is Jim."

Everyone murmured "hellos" and "how are yous" as I directed Jim to "shuffle up."

He shuffled the six decks. I took the third chair and could feel the eyes from the overhead security glued to the top of my head and the back of my neck. Jim offered me the cards to be cut, which I did with the plastic divider card that he handed me. I began by playing all six hands at $1,000 per hand. In ten minutes I was down $8,000. The shoe was exhausted, and the group around me, including Goldberg, were beside themselves with glee.

"So, Chance, you call this cheating?" asked Goldberg.

"No, it's called splashing. I'm losing a little cash to relax the heat, throwing you paranoid hawks off the scent. It's a grifter's term. I chalk it up to advertising." I smiled.

I turned to the small group of five people as Jim picked up the discards to shuffle.

"I wonder if you or any of your security people noticed anything different," I said.

"No," said the minister, who was all eyes and ears, glued to the scene by virtue of his vested interest in the outcome. "And

I'm sure they would have phoned down if the *eyes in the sky* had detected anything."

"Well, the first clue that something was out of whack should have been that I wasn't whining, bitching, moaning, or complaining about losing eight grand," I said and laughed.

While this conversation was going on, I calculated that it had taken about twenty seconds for Jim to shuffle the cards. When he was done, he offered me the cards to be cut. When I had done so, he took the block of cards and fitted them in the shoe.

"Let's cut to the chase, folks, because the game's all but over, and I've got a blonde parked with her motor running. Debbie's over at the Tilted Kilt Pub, and you are all invited for a celebratory drink after I win!"

"Mr. Daly, you sure are something. You say you are about to cheat us, but our eyes will be on you like white on rice," said the minister.

"Yes, sir. That's right. So crowd around, boys and girls, because it's showtime!"

And with that, I upped the bets to $10,000 per hand and won all six when the dealer dealt himself a sixteen and busted with a nine. On the next deal, he had an eighteen, and I won four hands with twenties, tied one, and lost one with a fourteen. The next hand, I won all six, including a blackjack. The deal after that, I played only three hands and stood on seventeen, fifteen, and twelve, and again the dealer busted, dealing himself a fourteen first and then hitting himself with a face card. In fifteen minutes I had their $200,000 in mock chips and their promise to pay me $397,000 hard cash.

"Well, I've seen it, but I don't believe it. Get the eyes down here," said Goldberg.

When they arrived, Goldberg was all over them.

"Did anybody see anything?" he demanded. "Security, did you see anything?"

He wheeled on me accusingly. "Chance, how do we know you didn't just get lucky? You could have just played us, and if you won, you got to sell us your materials. And if you lost, it wasn't the end of the world, because the materials didn't have a value to you anyway. Yeah, that's it. You just gambled."

As he glared at me, I stood up and faced everyone. I bowed, undid my belt, and dropped my pants. As soon as my trousers hit my shoes, everyone immediately jumped back two steps. They were stunned to see me standing there in my underwear with my pants draped around my ankles. It took a second to sink in, but they were even more dumbfounded to see, strapped to my right thigh, a small black keypad about the size of a very thin cell phone.

"Guys, may I present Viper? It's called Viper because it's deadly. And once it's locked on, it's game over. But don't be too hard on your security guys. Very few Vipers exist, and those who have them guard them and their technology with their lives. But let me give you a crash course about casino cheating, which should serve to illustrate just how vulnerable you are to thieves, cheaters, and new technology. To me, this technology is almost incomprehensible. But according to Johnny and our IT guys, even this Viper is rapidly becoming passé. That's how quickly the gaming world is changing.

"Anyway, here's how I cheated you," I said, pulling up my pants. "After the cards were dealt a few hands, I began to record their sequence on this pad hidden under my trousers. I just punched them into this specially designed keypad. This info was sent to a computer that is housed in a truck in the casino parking lot.

"But I only began to record the card sequence partway through the first shoe because at that point, Jim dropped a quarter-inch piece of knotted rubber band onto the discards. He had secreted it in the crotch between the thumb and first finger of his right hand. Paul, please hold out your hand, palms up. The tiny rubber band looked a lot like this." I passed my hand over his outstretched one and, while doing so, dropped a tiny piece of knotted rubber band onto his palm.

"This tiny bit of rubber, placed on top of the early discards, separated the early cards that had been dealt from the latter cards being played and recorded. In other words, the newly recorded discards were placed on top of the rubber band as the remaining cards were played. When the first card shoe was exhausted, Jim did a bunch of false shuffles and cuts to the recorded cards but left their sequence undisturbed. Then he legitimately shuffled the balance. The card moves are simple. They can be done easily by any dealer, or pitcher as they are referred to, or, in fact, by almost anybody who spends a lot of time handling cards. Interestingly, the false shuffles can be better detected at floor level than by the eyes in the sky, but I distracted you when I turned around to talk to you. I'm sure surveillance kept their eyes on the shuffle, but they couldn't see the manipulation from their vantage point overhead.

"The one bit of finesse that could have been problematic was when Jim offered me the stack of cards to cut. The purpose of the tiny piece of rubber band was to keep the early discards that had to actually be shuffled separate from the ones whose sequence had been recorded. The truly shuffled cards were on the top, so when Jim offered me the divider card to perform the cut, I had to place it perfectly in the tiny space created by the presence of the rubber band. He then took the bottom cards whose sequence had been recorded and placed them on top, completing the cut. Once I had hit the spot, it was game over. The computer had already analyzed all the odds and permutations, and Viper was transmitting all the information to me through an intracranial earpiece. All I had to do was follow instructions. Hit or stand. Hit or stand! So boys and girls, school's out! And the drinks are on me!"

Chapter Fourteen

"Give My Regards to Broadway," by George M. Cohan

*"New York State of Mind," written by Billy Joel and
performed by Barbra Streisand*

*"If You've Got the Money I've Got the Time,"
performed by Willie Nelson*
—Songs about the Big Apple

About a week after the blackjack game, the cheating-device demonstration, and the subsequent blowout celebration at the Tilted Kilt, I received an intriguing phone call from Bill Goldberg. He and I had ended up bonding over a couple of pool games where he was not quite good enough and a couple of dart games where he was unbelievably good. We had agreed that at some point in the future, we would have to get together for a golf game to determine the ultimate three-event champion. It was nice to get to know him a bit and to learn that he was actually a pretty cool guy despite being a total suit. If there was a downside to that night, it was that we probably had a few too many libations. But what the hell, it's not every day that a guy can pick up $397,000 in a single blackjack game, even if I did have to resort to cheating.

The phone call wasn't totally unexpected, nor was the subject matter. After the initial greeting and small talk, Goldberg said,

"Chance, I've had an opportunity to speak with our chairman, Bob Findlay. I shared with him how hugely impressed I've been with you. He was, of course, intrigued with my description of your demonstration of the Viper, but he was especially dismayed when I told him about your opinion of our casino operations.

"Because of the alarm bells you set off, he and I are both hoping you would come up to New York and meet him and a few members of the board of directors. We hope to also have our new King's Own general manager here, so it would be a good opportunity for us all to get together."

"Bill, as much as I appreciate the opportunity to meet everyone, and I would love to have a bite of lunch with you, I'm really not keen on flying all the way to New York just for a meet and greet," I said.

"I understand, Chance, but it's only a two-and-a-half-hour flight, and I can promise that you won't be disappointed. We have some ideas that you may find intriguing. Tell you what— why don't you bring that beautiful bride with you at our expense? We'll put you up at our flagship hotel here in New York as our guests. I know Debbie would have a wonderful time taking in the sights. How about coming in next Thursday and staying through the weekend? We'll have our meetings on Friday, and if it's not an imposition, I'll bring my wife into the city on Saturday, and the four of us can take in a play on Broadway. Maybe we can even get tickets to see *Jersey Boys*."

"Jesus, Bill, did you sell used cars while putting yourself through school?" I laughed. "You sure make it sound inviting. Let me talk to Debbie, and I'll get back to you in the morning. And thanks for the invitation and the kind words."

The following Thursday found us on the plane to New York. And as bad as Deb's new aversion to flying was, it still wasn't enough to deter her from the prospect of a New York shopping excursion. I couldn't help but think somewhat ruefully that with her *black belt* in shopping, she was going to put a sizable dent in that $1 million break fee.

Goldberg had booked us into the Essex House Hotel on Central Park South, and it was everything their website said it would be. "Debbie, my girl, this suite is something out of the movies!" I exclaimed as we entered. It had a huge bedroom, a formal living room, and its own dining room. But the coup de grace was a six-passenger hot tub with a magnificent cloud-high view of Central Park. Palatial was the only word to describe it.

A little jazzed from the flight, we decided to take a brief stroll to shake off the kinks. We were only gone twenty minutes, when Deb said that she had had enough walking and that it was time for us to return to our room. We—make that she—decided that there was nothing outside the hotel that mattered to her that evening and that it would be in our collective best interest to have dinner alone in our beautiful suite (which we did) and then have a soak in the hot tub and drink champagne (which we did). Then Deb told me once again how proud she was of me and how much she loved me. Then she rewarded me for being her true love in a manner that women have been employing for thousands of years. I made a mental note to put Deb in charge of all future plans.

Our Friday-morning meeting at the offices of Diamond Resorts International in midtown Manhattan started promptly at 9:00 a.m. My lovely wife had insisted that I wear the new suit she had just bought me, and also a tie. The meeting, with all the pinstripe attendees, looked like a Brooks Brothers convention.

After meeting the new King's Own Resort General Manager JoAnn Rider, introductions and coffee were passed around, and

Chairman Bob Findlay gave me a brief intro to Diamond Resorts. Initially I didn't let on that I had reviewed their financials and had done considerable additional research on the Internet. But after a couple of my too-penetrating questions, Goldberg said, "With respect, Mr. Chairman, I'm getting the impression that Chance is fairly well up to speed on our operations."

I smiled and said, "Well, the truth is that I did take the opportunity to learn a little about Diamond Resorts, and may I say I am very impressed. And had it been otherwise, Debbie and I probably wouldn't have made the trip."

I was fairly well versed in their global operations. In addition, as part of our due diligence process, Norm, Johnny, Barry (our numbers guy), and I had visited each of their casino operations, learning in Aruba and in the Dominican Republic the magnitude of some of their problems and how badly Diamond Resorts was getting ripped off. Prompted by questions by the chairman over the next few hours, I laid out our findings. Understandably, everyone assembled was interested in my revelations.

We then dispersed for a quick bite of lunch and reconvened an hour later.

"Chance, would you consider joining our corporate fold?" said Mr. Findlay once I had finished. "Bill is right. You would be a perfect fit for our organization. We need someone at ten thousand feet to help us protect ourselves from both internal and external skulduggery."

"Thank you, Mr. Findlay. I'm honored by your offer, and I must admit that it doesn't come as a complete surprise. We knew that we weren't being invited up here just for sightseeing. My wife, Debbie, and I have discussed the possibility that you might want our involvement on some level, and may I say that we are intrigued. But before we consider the possibility seriously,

I'd like to know where Diamond Resorts stands philosophically on a number of issues. Would you allow me to ask a few questions?—because knowing your corporate philosophy would be fundamental to my involvement and my ultimate value to your corporation." Without waiting for a reply, I went on. "The casino industry is unique. The raison d'être is to take money from guests, while hoping they will enjoy the process. There are a couple of crass ways to describe the challenge, but the terminology is not for mixed company." I laughed.

"Oh come on, Chance, we're all big boys and girls here. What do you mean?" demanded Findlay.

Trapped, I glanced over to Bill Goldberg for support. He only smiled and shrugged his shoulders, so I went on. "Well, as I see it, your task is to ensure that guests think that the fucking they're getting is worth the fucking they're getting!"

There were laughs all around as I went on. "Well, it's true. You want to relieve your guests of just enough of their cash that they can still chalk up their loss to entertainment. But you don't want them to feel they've been screwed or abused...which brings me to the first question—have you discussed casino profit expectations with your partners? It's hugely important to your relationship with them that all parties agree on things as basic as hold and win percentages on your slot machines. Both parties also need to agree on payouts on the Craps tables, even to whether you want single or double zeros on the roulette wheels. The vig, or the win percentage, on single zero is two and three-fifths percent, while it's five and five-nineteenths percent for double zeros. One profit philosophy can be efficacious; another can be abusive."

"And what do you suggest?" asked Bill Goldberg.

"Bill, I'm not going to stand here and fire off a bunch of percentages and numbers. That's not what you want from me.

Another day, another time, I will relate our in-depth analysis to you and provide specific recommendations. The owners can then make the final determination based on their combined corporate philosophy and their profit expectations. I can tell you, though, that I come from the school of 'let's give the guest good value for their entertainment dollar.' It doesn't do a lot to jack up your profitability initially, but long term it's the only way to go.

"Not incidentally, I can also help you compensate for what might be perceived in some quarters, as this reduced casino profit strategy. I can also help you prevent profit erosion and even stop you from being robbed the way you are now. My hope would be that because of these savings, the powers that be would quickly see the merit in giving their guests a better bang for their buck by reducing the casino's vig to a more user-friendly level. It's trite to say, but the more your guests enjoy their vacation experience, the more likely it is that they will keep returning. As I said to Bill in San Vida, if a tourist feels like he or she has been ripped off, chances are you'll never get them back. Nor are they likely to recommend your resort to their friends.

I call this Chance's Law of Diminishing Return. But there is no question in my mind that the more a casino operator turns up the take on the slot machines in pursuit of 'just a little more profit,' the more they run the risk of alienating their casino guests and turning them off completely.

"I think we would agree that most guests or players mentally budget how much they're going to lose at the casino. We also know that in all likelihood, the casino is going to get all of that budgeted amount, and probably a little more. Well, if the casino is going to get all the money anyway, then why not let your guest play a little longer? And in the process, let them have a little more fun. Going this route, you can be sure that word will get around that you have loose slots or loose table games, and you will absolutely attract more players."

"Chance, you are everything Bill said you were and I couldn't agree more. So to my earlier question, would you be interested in coming on board and helping us in this regard?" asked Findlay.

"Well, thank you for your consideration, but before responding, let me ask you and your board members just a few more things. I believe it's important that we look one another in the eye here so that we are completely in sync, if and when I do come on board. And the marching orders I'd like to discuss aren't necessarily just for me. They're for Bill and JoAnn's benefit as well."

"Sure, Chance, go ahead."

"Operating a casino profitably occasionally requires harsh measures, particularly when responding to the actions of cheaters and thieves." I waited as this sunk in. "I know I can work with Bill, and my instincts are that I can work with JoAnn as well, and I have no desire to get into specifics here and now. But personally, I believe a casino needs to protect itself from cheaters by discouraging their return once they have been caught. The best way to do this is to extract an ounce of flesh—not a pound of flesh like the boys in Vegas used to do and certainly not like Benny Binion's Horseshoe or the Stardust used to do. Those casinos took corporal punishment to the extreme, with soundproof rooms where cheaters were taken and beaten and hands smashed with ball-peen hammers. Very harsh deterrents indeed.

"I don't believe in those extremely harsh measures, but I do believe in *some* punishment. Harsh enough that cheaters quickly understand that it can be painful to try to rip off any casino under my watch. Again, I believe this is essential for the successful operation of a casino. And if I'm charged with the responsibility of operating a profitable business, then that would be my MO requirement. Does anybody have a problem with that?"

There were murmurs of acquiescence and somewhat tacit agreement all around.

"There are also a few less intrusive measures I would adopt for management and staff."

"Such as?" ventured JoAnn.

"I believe in using lie detectors," I said.

There was a chorus of agreement as everyone was relieved to be steering away from the less savory thought of cheaters being subjected to physical punishment.

Somebody even remarked, "Yeah, that can be a great idea. It's too bad the laws in the United States sometimes restrict their use."

"Well, the truth is that many of the truly bad guys are savvy to the fact that lie detectors can often be fooled. But I would want to employ them more as a warning tool, regardless."

"What do you mean the lie detector can be fooled?" asked JoAnn.

"There are a couple of pretty simple methods. One way is for the person taking the test to create some false positives early in the Q&A. It doesn't work always, but it does often, and it's actually fairly easy for a bad guy with a vested interest in preserving his status or his health to beat the machine by creating these baseline deviations. The subject simply provides incorrect answers to the initial questions that the technicians have to ask when calibrating their machines prior to conducting the lie-detector test.

"Another way to throw the machines off is for the subject to inflict pain on themselves when responding to a question. To do this they usually have a needle partially stuck into some sensitive part of their anatomy, and when they have to answer, they press on that painful point, which creates false negatives on the machine. Of course, not everybody can fool the machine every time. But some can. But be that as it may, to me, the greatest value of the polygraph is when everyone becomes aware that it *may* be used at *any* time for *any* reason.

"And if someone fails, they're out. No questions asked or answered—they're gone! Please realize that the polygraph is just *another club in management's tool bag,* but I wanted to ascertain your thoughts. I'm now satisfied that we understand one another. So please allow my wife Debbie and I, time to consider your proposal. We will give it serious thought and will provide our answer next week.

"But I will leave you with a couple of final thoughts. First, whether it is by me or someone like me, you need to perform a complete overhaul of your casino operations. Secondly, I promise you that if you embrace the improvements to your gaming operations as per my recommendations, Diamond Resorts will earn millions of dollars each year in additional profits *and* will provide a more meaningful and pleasurable experience for your resort guests. And that's a guarantee."

Bill Goldberg walked me to the elevator, and we made plans to meet with the wives the following day. We decided we would meet at our hotel before going to the restaurant where Bill had made reservations. The Per Se was one of New York's few restaurants with three Michelin stars, and Debbie was over the moon when she checked out their website. And when I told her that later we were going to see the musical

Jersey Boys, she once again rewarded me for being her husband. There must be something in the New York water. It was like being on our honeymoon.

Saturday dawned warm and sunny. As we wandered around Times Square and Central Park on such a beautiful day, Debbie spoke of how blessed we were to have such an idyllic life. "Chance, there's something I'd like you to consider for me. What would you think about having another child?"

Of course, I should have seen this coming. The entire vibe was just so positive and warm. What could I say but, "Sure, sweetheart. If that's what you want, I think we'd better get back to our hotel and start right now!" I thought I had made a funny joke, but I apparently Debbie took it quite seriously. She grabbed my hand and propelled us the two blocks back to our hotel. If we hadn't had early dinner reservations with the Goldbergs, we might have killed ourselves.

Four o'clock found us in the bar just off the hotel lobby. We had wandered in just as Bill and his wife Virginia arrived. It was a little like old home week for Debbie and Bill. They were glad to say hi and catch up, but once Deb and Virginia met, Bill and I could have been on the moon for all they cared. Debbie could start a conversation in an empty room, and with Virginia, she had found her match—and her kindred spirit. Virginia was an absolute knockout and as articulate as she was beautiful. They were immediately on the same page and off to the nonstop talking Olympics.

We didn't sit around the bar for long, as Debbie was no longer drinking any alcohol. She couldn't resist telling everyone the reason. Then Virginia asked, "And how long have you been pregnant?" Debbie responded, "If we're lucky, about two hours!" provoking considerable laughter.

We strolled the block and a half to the Per Se and couldn't help but be impressed with the urban beauty and the hustle and bustle of the city. Once we were seated and drinks ordered, the task of placing our orders was next on the agenda. After poring over the menu for far too long, Debbie and I eventually abdicated the ordering of dinner to our hosts. It was a damn good thing we did. We were rubes in this league. It turned out to be an extraordinary ten-course dinner event.

Bill explained that meals like this should be viewed as fine art, but rather than art on canvas, this was art for your eyes, your nose, and especially your taste buds. Clearly, Goldberg was a foodie. Each course was accompanied by a small serving of a specially paired wine supposedly designed "to elevate the flavors in the food to create a unique taste experience." Debbie briefly reconsidered her possible pregnancy but remained firm. The table was set with more glassware and silverware than a Bloomingdale's warehouse.

The first course came out as four servers placed the silver-domed plates in front of us and, with an orchestrated flourish, removed the four domes simultaneously. One of the servers announced that the minuscule serving of glimmering space food on our plates was, in fact, a "sabayon of pearl tapioca with Island Creek oysters and sterling white sturgeon caviar" and that our paired wine was "an Henri Boillot 2005 Batard-Montrachet" white French Burgundy. I wasn't exactly sure how to eat this or even which utensils I should use, so we waited for Virginia to start and followed her lead.

From the first bite, it was clear that the flavors were like nothing I had ever eaten before. And my first sip of wine almost had me thinking there was some kind of taste-enhancing chemical reaction being created. Two bites later, our plates were whisked away, and the next course of silver domes and sample wine magically appeared. Eight courses later, after *velouté, moulard*, duck roti, and poached lobster, and wines from France, Spain, and Italy, and after the third dessert course, the feast was over. Bill looked at us all and said, "Where do you want to go for our after-theater meal?" We all laughed as we held our bellies.

When the check arrived, I made a vain attempt to grab it, but Bill wouldn't have any part of it. I protested weakly, saying, "You guys are taking us to see *Jersey Boys*, and you won't let us pay for our tickets. At least let us pick up the dinner check."

"No way, Chance. You are our guests and the guest of Mr. Findlay, and we are pleased that you came all the way to New York to visit."

I looked at Debbie for some support, but she just shrugged her shoulders. Virginia did the same. What could I do but say, "Well, guys, I guess Jimmy Stewart was right. Yes, Virginia, there is a Santa Claus."

Good joke, good laugh, great time.

And I was lucky that he outwrestled me for the check. I saw the bill. It was more than four thousand dollars. *Four Thousand!* Not wanting to appear too much like a country bumpkin, I asked Bill if I could maybe take, or even buy, a menu to take home as a souvenir. In truth, I wanted to show it to Norm and the troops, and I knew that without proof they would never believe me.

"Chance!" Bill laughed. "No need to even think of purloining a menu. We've spent enough here over the years that I'm sure they'll give us one. And if they don't…then and only then, we'll steal it!"

It took us about fifteen minutes to waddle our way down Broadway, arriving at our third-row seats just minutes before the production started. I couldn't help but think, *Man, oh man, this is a long way from the back alleys of West Toronto.*

Chapter Fifteen

Often the best luck occurs when preparation meets opportunity.
—Seymour Harris, Rancho Mirage, California

Dear Mr. Findlay,

My wife, Debbie, and I had a most memorable time in New York. It was wonderful to meet you and your board of directors and to be hosted by Mr. and Mrs. Goldberg on Saturday evening. We want to express our thanks, and we want you to know how much we appreciate your kind and generous hospitality.

    Considering your offer has proved most interesting and has caused considerable soul searching. I have ultimately concluded that because the casino-related needs of Diamond Resorts are so broad in scope, that it would be in our collective best interests for me to propose an alternative that is far more encompassing. In my professional opinion, you need more than just the undersigned in the capacity of general manager of casino operations.

    Your greatest need is a cultural and systemic makeover. The cancer of theft is endemic throughout all your casino operations that we studied. Drastic measures should be taken immediately. But while we all realize that all casino operations must be brought up to acceptable performance standards as soon as practically possible, it has to be recognized that to do so will require new, trusted, and skilled management. One person, namely myself, simply can't do it alone. Nor can improvements be brought about in any sort of reasonable time frame without skilled and trusted support personnel. In that regard, and as good fortune would have it, there are a number of my former Toronto-based associates here in San Vida. They worked for and with me in our Toronto card room, casino and gaming operations, and all came to Balboa in anticipation of my acquisition of the King's Own Casino and Resort. Now that I am no longer completing the acquisition, they are under-deployed. As such they are immediately available.

On the other hand, I have family considerations, and I'm just not as inclined to jump on and off airplanes as I might have been even just a few years ago.

Therefore, I would like to propose an alternative to your offer that would, in my opinion, better meet the broader needs of Diamond Resorts and also the specific needs of the King's Own Casino, while allowing me to base my involvement from our permanent home location, which has now become San Vida.

I propose that as an integral part of a far more encompassing plan, that I will undertake to see that the San Vida casino is properly staffed and managed. I would further recommend that we use the King's Own casino as an operating model for others in your hotel and casino system. With San Vida as a quasi-training facility, we would then be in a position to bring in new management and staff for, and possibly from, the other casinos in your system to be trained, and trained properly.

Concurrent with bringing San Vida on stream, my key personnel and I will also move rapidly to stop the financial hemorrhaging currently taking place at the other casinos throughout the Diamond Resorts International organization. The goal will be to bring all casino performances and profits up to industry standards in very short order.

Clearly, this is a compromise response to your offer, but I believe it will address both the compelling needs of Diamond Resorts and also those of the undersigned. I will look forward to your response, and thank you once again for your consideration.

Sincerely,

C. N. Daly

Chapter Sixteen

In business and in life, we are who others think we are.
—Chance Daly

Two days later I was offered the position of vice president of casino operations for Diamond Resorts International, with a virtual carte blanche to do whatever I thought necessary to improve the performance of their casinos. It occurred to me that I had been preparing for this role my entire life.

Three weeks later I phoned Bill and said, "We're having a bonding session here in San Vida next week—would you like to join us? In addition to JoAnn Rider, some of our senior management team and their wives, are going to join us for a spousal meet-and-greet soiree. It would be great for you to bring Virginia down as well. She would be a welcome addition, and it would be a nice opportunity for you to meet the team who are involved in your casino operations. Of course, the gals won't be sitting in on our meetings, but I know Debbie would love to see Virginia and catch up on the zillion things they've just got to talk about."

With plans to put the casino back in operation on October 15, and the phased opening of about 20 percent of the rooms on November 1, it was 24/7 for everyone. JoAnn was immersed in assembling her resort-management team, and with about sixty days to go before the opening of the casino and showroom, we were fully deployed hiring and training dealers, cocktail waitresses, and cage and surveillance staff. We also needed to get our arms around the other casino operations in the southern Caribbean. We were as busy as one-armed truck drivers with crabs, but we loved it.

While Debbie hosted the spouses at our home in Balboan Estates, I convened a meeting in the casino, which was rapidly rounding back into shape. Key personnel in attendance included two new casino pit bosses, a casino manager and a count-room manager, and my battle-hardened execs from our Toronto CIA club, including Norm Fiske, Barry Denton, and Johnny Anderson. Hotel GM JoAnn Rider joined us as well, as did Bill Goldberg.

"Ladies and gentlemen," I began, "to reiterate, we have an opportunity to create a casino operation here in San Vida that will be the model for Diamond Resort International casinos throughout the entire Caribbean. Personnel and management from elsewhere will come here to learn how to manage their casinos and how to protect their operations from fraud and theft. They will employ our systems, style, and culture, and we will lead. We have a blank piece of paper to basically comport ourselves as we see fit and manage as we see fit. And the reason that we are being given this latitude and opportunity is due in large part to the discoveries of Johnny and Barry.

"As you know, during our due diligence process, Johnny, Barry, and I spent considerable time checking out the other eight DR casinos. We have determined that significant internal fraud and outright theft is prevalent in virtually every DR casino that we visited."

"Chance, for the benefit of those of us who are not totally steeped in the casino industry, would you just take a couple of minutes to give us a quick description of what they found, just so we're all—at least a little bit—on the same page?" asked JoAnn.

"Yes, of course," I replied. "Good idea. But before I do, let me say again…what you learn here is strictly confidential. We have huge issues elsewhere, and if others hear that we're on to them, it would make our job double tough. Understood?"

I could see agreement all around.

"In one casino, it has been determined that some blackjack games had been rigged in favor of the house. Ripping off players became necessary because the dealer and pit-boss thieves were stealing such large amounts of money that they need to mask their thefts. As you know, dependent on the volume of play, each table is supposed to earn a profit from the losses of the players. The *casino win* should be fairly predictable depending on the amount that the players bet, but because so much money is being stolen, the thieves have to cheat players at an egregious rate to cover their tracks."

"How are they doing it?" asked JoAnn.

"Well, unfortunately, that can be more simple than most would imagine. Casino personnel, and arguably maybe even management, have been using the same method that has been used on cruise ships for years. Everybody here is aware that in blackjack, when the remaining cards in a shoe are rich in ten counts, that is, tens, jacks, queens, and kings, then that favors the player and savvy players increase their bets accordingly. Conversely, they reduce the amount of their bets when there is an overabundance of small cards, because that situation favors the house.

"That is the essence of card counting. Card counters increase the amount of their bets when the odds are in their favor—that is, when there is a disproportionate number of ten counts remaining in the shoe—and they reduce the amount of their bets when there is an overabundance of small cards remaining. Well, in an

Aruba casino, Johnny and Barry determined that in the six-deck shoes, the bad guys were taking out twelve ten-count cards and were substituting those cards with twelve twos, threes, and fours. There are three hundred and twelve cards in a six-deck shoe, and of those, ninety-six are supposed to be ten counts. As a result the odds favored the casino and the "table win" was much greater and that allowed management to steal that much more without being detected. And who would notice? Nobody, that's who! So we, and DR owe a debt of gratitude to our intrepid investigators, Barry, Johnny, outstanding job! Well done!"

There were murmurs of exclamation and agreement all around as I continued. "Our guys also found a magnetic roulette ball that was being used at the roulette table, but that's a little more mundane. But there is a real ballsy rip-off that is still going on at the Dominican Republic casino. And I remind you that the bad guys don't know that we know, so everything you are now hearing should be treated as completely confidential. We're going to come down on them hard in three days, and we don't want to tip them off. It's going to take considerable effort, and it's imperative that we find out just how high up this very sophisticated fraud goes.

"Also, as we all know, the count room is the heart of any casino. All coins and cash from the slot machines should theoretically make their way from the slot machines into locked boxes and then transported to the count room where the cash is counted under camera surveillance, and the coins are weighed, counted, rolled, recorded, and then delivered back to the casino floor to be sold to players. However with thanks to Johnny and Barry, we have determined that *someone* has built and installed an extra change booth in the middle of the casino. There the coins are resold to casino players, and the cash goes out in the purses of the change booth employees. Slick as could be but not too original. You recall the movie *Casino?* The story of the Stardust Hotel in Vegas? Robert De Niro played the part of Lefty Rosenthal, the head of Casino operations. Joe Pesci played the Mafia boss, Anthony Spilotro. Lefty was the emissary of the Chicago mob and was sent to Vegas to watch over their interests, which included the Stardust. His arrival occurred just before the FBI began to scrutinize closely the operations of all Las Vegas casinos.

"For years, the casino count rooms had been the source of millions of dollars of unreported profits that bagmen would deliver back home to the Mob undetected by the IRS. However, once the FBI arrived, Lefty had to devise a way to keep the unreported profits flowing. He did this by setting up extra change booth islands on the casino floor. These change booths were off the reporting grid, and that allowed Lefty et al, to hijack slot-machine coins by the kazillion. Once he had control of the coins, it was simple to sell them to slot players for bills, and the resulting flow of cash went back to Chicago, unreported for years. So guys, we've got a real challenge on our hands. We need to figure out who the bad guys are, get them out, and get new, clean people in as seamlessly as possible. We're doing that almost immediately, but right now we have many competing priorities with the opening of this casino and the simultaneous need to establish new systems and procedures for all casinos. JoAnn, any more questions? None? OK, that should get us all on the same song sheet, so now let's get down to business.

"I'm going to begin by discussing equipment and systems for our new San Vida casino operation. Obviously, we want to make certain everything is properly installed, tested, and fully operational for our grand opening.

"First, we need to update our surveillance cameras. We need to get the new Camonix system that records everything digitally, can hold fourteen days of film, does freeze frame, and incorporates watermark technology that highlights any foul play or image altering after the fact. Incidentally, it's the only system that will stand up in court.

"Next, we want to join and fully participate in the DDS program. That stands for Disguise Detection System. It allows participating casinos to share photos of cheaters, grafters, crooks, and those who have been barred from casinos for one reason or another. To give you a sense of the magnitude, the last time I checked, there were over seven thousand perps on file, whose facial features have been committed to computer imaging. This won't totally protect us from all the disguised crooks, but it's a start. And, by the way, I want each of our greeters, as well as our cocktail hostesses, to take an online course in disguise application to help hone their disguise-detection skills."

"Greeters?" questioned Norm.

"Yeah, it's in keeping with an old Las Vegas tradition. Back in the day, a number of retired boxing champions were employed as Las Vegas casino greeters. Joe Louis, Rocky Marciano, and even Jack Dempsey, who worked for Al Capone for a while, were all greeters. Their job was to stand near the front door and welcome folks as they entered. Many people coming into the casino would find it fun to stop, chat, and have their photo taken with a former boxing champion. It's a nice touch and a not-too-subtle reminder that there are forces to be reckoned with in the event someone gets out of line.

"I have two candidates in mind to be our greeters. First, our local Ozzie Smith, who can charm the birds out of a tree. He has a great personality and is well known to locals as a person not to be trifled with. I think he would make an excellent choice. Norm, would you mind speaking to Sy Goldstein to get his thoughts? Sy and Ozzie have become buddies over the last few months, so I would welcome his input on the idea. The other person I have in mind is George Chuvalo. George was the heavyweight boxing champion of Canada for over twenty years, and as anyone who has seen him knows, not only is he as big as a house, but he also combines that incredible physique with a warm, friendly demeanor.

"I knew him well years ago when I used to take bets and play cards at the car lots along Bloor Street in Toronto. George used to play in the Hearts games and was a real sharp card player. If he'll consider taking the job, he would be perfect to help us create the image we want to convey. I'll contact him, and Norm, please get back to me after you've spoken with Sy about Ozzie.

"Also, we want to incentivize all our people to be constantly on the lookout for crooks, creeps, frauds, and cheaters. We want all our employees to be eligible and enthusiastic about receiving a bonus in the event they finger a perp. Barry, I'd like you to create some sort of an incentive system that we can use to reward our employees. And I was being only partially facetious the other day when I said we should photograph and permanently ban everyone who comes into our casino during the first sixty days of operation. It is probable that every crook and cheater in the western hemisphere is going to try us on when we open our doors. And believe me, partially trained and inexperienced casino personnel are no match for professional cheaters. So it's our job to make sure that the interests of the casino and the King's Own Resort are well protected.

"As part of our training program, role playing will be an important tool. So when our trainees have completed their program, I'd like us to hold an event, simulating actual game and casino conditions. We'll invite the service clubs—the Kiwanis, Rotary, the Optimist Club, all of them—and the schools and churches to a charity night. All those entities are constantly searching for ways to generate extra funds, so this will be the perfect opportunity for them.

"Participating schools can promote the charity function to their Parent Teachers Associations and the churches to their congregations, and the Service Clubs are great at getting behind an event and supporting it. We'll provide the attendees with play money and chips that winners can use at the end of the night to buy prizes, and the participating groups can charge admission and hold silent auctions, and we'll provide the casino dealers and staff at no cost to them. Of course, the big benefit to us is that we will have the opportunity to monitor the performance of our staff under real game conditions. I think we'll ask Debbie to take on the role of being the go-to person to coordinate this. This is right up her alley. Any thoughts, ideas, or comments?"

"Chance, it might be a pretty overwhelming task with only a few weeks to go until our grand opening, so if you don't have any objections, perhaps I should give her a hand," offered Johnny.

"Great idea, and thanks. You and Debbie have the ball. The next agenda item is safety and security. We want to constantly reinforce to all staff that our role includes protecting players and patrons from any and all criminal element. Patrons should feel secure from the time they arrive at our parking lot until they leave our property. That means that we want to have absolutely no dark corners anywhere inside, outside, or anywhere around our perimeter. Don't forget that if the bad guys can rob golfers on the golf course, they can rob our casino winners. And winners are most susceptible when they are returning to their vehicles with a pocket full of cash. Make sure robberies *do not happen*. In fact, now that it's on the table, please instruct the cashiers and cage personnel to always ask anyone cashing out for more than five hundred dollars if they would like an escort to their vehicle.

"And inside the casino, I want everyone from box men to cocktail waitresses to pay particular attention to the actions of spectators as well as players. It's going to be a fact that, particularly on weekends, we will have an abundance of desirable, ostensibly available women, visiting the casino. Back in their hometowns, they are secretaries, bank tellers, librarians, whatever, but when they get off the plane, they become different women. And the most dangerous are going to be the part-time amateurs. Yes, they're here to have a good time, but most of all, they are opportunists. And the most prevalent of the lot will be chip croppers."

"Who or what is that?" asked JoAnn.

"They are the gals and guys who mostly work the Craps and roulette tables. Essentially, they crop, scoop, or otherwise steal chips from players at every opportunity. They usually position themselves so that when players beside them reach over to place their bets, they grab their chips. This type of crook is as nimble and talented as David Copperfield or Penn and Teller. They use an array of devices, one of the most popular being a simple magnetic bracelet. These are extremely effective because they look like any other piece of jewelry. Most casino chips are made of a clay that contains a metal compound, and any magnet passed over the chips will cause them to leap up as much as four inches and attach themselves to the underside of a wrist or arm. This happens in a flash and is virtually undetectable. Also to aid distraction, they use magicians' holdout pouches, spilled drinks, and big boobs."

Laughter all around.

I smiled. "You get the picture. We want our employees to understand that we are the good guys. The thieves, cheaters, crooks, and creeps are the bad guys. It's us against them, and we need to win all day, every day.

"All employees also need to know that they will be asked to take lie-detector tests from time to time. We know that approximately 34 percent of thefts in resorts, hotels, and casinos are carried out by staff. We need to ward off any pilfering before it happens. Also, according to Interpol, US passports now bring about fifteen thousand dollars on the black market. So at the front desk, until we get the room safes installed, we want to strongly suggest to our guests that they utilize our corporate hotel safe to store their valuables, including passports. And in that regard, all management personnel are invited to have your passports and valuables placed in the safe as well."

It was a productive meeting and weekend. While our corporate meeting was going on, Debbie, Marilyn, and Rylee had hosted and totally captivated our guests. They had a lovely Saturday afternoon lounging around our pool. And when the rest of us returned from our meeting, everyone freshened up, and we went to the Stoned Crab for dinner.

Despite the great food and beautiful sunset, the evening was badly marred by Rylee's reaction to the shark feeding. She absolutely freaked. And I don't blame her. The spectacle of those huge sharks crashing up and out of the water only fifteen feet below us, fighting for bones and carcasses bothered even me. And *I* knew we were safe. But for a little kid it was understandably terrifying, and I was annoyed with myself for subjecting her to the frenzy of blood, guts, and carnage.

Grandmother Marilyn rescued the evening somewhat by

taking Rylee home when she proved inconsolable. But fifteen minutes after they left, Debbie, who felt as awful as I did, couldn't stand it, so she made her apologies and left as well. All in all, a not-so-nice way to end what otherwise would have been a great day.

Chapter Seventeen

A true professional gambler doesn't like to gamble. He is always careful to ensure that the odds are in his favor, before making any bet. And his belief isn't broken when he loses. He didn't win? It's not the end of the world. Tomorrow's another day, and the immutable law of averages will always prevail.
Winning is only a matter of time.
—Chance Daly

The charity casino night was a huge success. Debbie had been awesome in enlisting the support of the organizations. She and Johnny had gone around and personally visited all the priests, ministers, rabbis, schools, and YMCA and service clubs to explain the opportunity. Often Debbie would take Rylee with her. I mean, who was ever going to question the intentions of a mom, accompanied by her beautiful little blond-haired, blue-eyed, three-year-old sidekick?

Participating organizations raised a combined $48,000, so they were delighted. We were satisfied as well, as we had had our chance to monitor the performance of our dealers and casino staff. But it was quite a wake-up call for our management team. They knew that I was more than just a little disappointed with some of the oversight and just plain sloppy management decisions that had been made; and I didn't let the guys off easy for what I considered to be the equivalent of dumb rookie mistakes.

The day after the charity casino night, I assembled our key personnel, asking JoAnn to sit in as well. I was a little cranky as I began: "I think it's a damn good thing we had our charity rehearsal event before our soft opening. It's obvious that many of our dealers are ill-prepared to deal with the public. Frankly, I thought our dealer's school and training programs would have produced a much higher caliber of personnel. Did some of those dealers even attend our dealer's school? A number of them wouldn't have lasted out their first shift in Vegas.

"I even saw one blackjack dealer looking at his hole card every time he dealt a hand. And I don't mean when his up card was an ace or a ten count. I mean *every time!* And this was before the players even had the opportunity to make their decision to hit or stay. Tell me why he would do that unless he was planning on cheating the players. It's either that or he doesn't understand the first thing about being a dealer. His name's Jamal. Get him back in our dealer school and put him on notice that one more screw-up and he's toast.

"Also, I don't know where my brain was when I let this purchase order go through for chairs with rattan backs. Have them retrofitted. All casino chairs need to have solid backs. In fact, as long as you're having them retrofitted, have a thin sheet of tin placed between the frame at the back and the leather. Cheaters are always searching for hole card tells, and they are now using transmittal devices so powerful that we need to block their signals whenever we can.

"And where were our collective heads when we had those overhead surveillance cameras installed? Didn't anyone notice that they have bright red lights about the size of a dime that come on whenever the cameras are being activated? Anybody planning to cheat would notice immediately when an area is being watched. So either make the damn things stay on all the time or simply take the bulbs out. Now we've got two weeks to clean up our act. Any other business?"

"Yes, Chance, we've had some new thoughts about the casino layout," Norm intoned. "We've been kicking around the location of the slot machines relative to the Craps and blackjack tables and the entrance to the casino. We've concluded that the way we have the floor plan laid out now, with the slots at the back of the casino and along the walls, is old school. We've reviewed the layout of the newer Las Vegas casinos, and they are placing more slots at, and near, the entrances and moving the gaming tables toward the rear. We know that there are a growing number of slot players, and we want to make it easier for them to get to the machines when they enter the casino. This would also give us a second chance to get their play when they are leaving the casino. It might also serve to motivate the more casual players or neophytes to play. You know, the lookers—those folks who often stick their head in the door just to take a look. Those casual visitors might be intimidated by gaming tables but would possibly be more inclined to stick a quarter in a machine if some were at the front and more readily accessible."

I nodded. "Is everybody on board with this?" I asked.

When everybody murmured their support for the idea, I said, "Draw up a revised floor plan, and let me take a look at it. Anything else?"

"Yes," said Norm. "On a positive note, the idea of bringing in Chuvalo and hiring Ozzie has been well received. Did you see the folks crowd around George? He was the perfect host. And Ozzie was the consummate professional. I swear he must have attended the Dale Carnegie School and majored in How to Win Friends and Influence People. The two of them could not have been better representatives. Also, Ozzie asked me to tell you how much he appreciates the opportunity you gave him. He said there aren't a lot of jobs for an ex-con in Balboa, and he's grateful for the chance. That's quite a statement coming from someone who was once purported to be one of the most dangerous people on the island. And let me tell you, it's sure nice to have him in our tent pissing out rather than outside our tent pissing in.

"Incidentally, Ozzie did have to cool out one of our bartenders. Ozzie said this Romeo was hitting on the female customers. He said everybody calls the guy *Carpenter* because he tries to nail every gal he meets. Ozzie told him to cut it out, but the bartender insisted that the gals love his repartee. He says it even improves his tips. He was saying that he tells all the gals that even Ray Charles could see they are beautiful, and that he'd like to go to bed with them. He says he figures that 90 percent of the time, he has a fifty-fifty chance of getting laid!"

"Jeez!" I laughed. "The guy sounds like Yogi Berra. I don't know what the hell he means, but we can't have that type of conduct, so put him on notice to clean up his act. No ifs, ands, or buts. And tell Ozzie in particular to keep an eye on him."

"OK, Chance, but the bottom line is that it was a great decision to bring both Ozzie and George on board. It's working really well."

"Well, thanks, Norm. That's nice to hear. And I appreciate the comment, but that doesn't let anyone off the hook. We still need to improve our performance. We've only got a few days before the opening, so let's get at it."

"Just one last thing Chance. That was a nice gesture on your part to make the hotel safe available to our executive personnel. They all know how busy you are, and for you to look out for them was much appreciated."

"Nice to hear," I said. "Did everybody put their passports in the safe?"

"Yeah," Norm said. "Everybody except Johnny."

I said, "What's up with him? That's strange."

Norm shrugged. "Incidentally, the other day I saw him and four or five well-dressed, hard-looking Latinos having drinks over at the Tropicana. If I didn't know better, I'd think he was trying to avoid me. When I wandered in, he didn't look too happy to see me. Certainly he made no move to introduce me."

"Any idea what's going on?"

"Nope."

It was probably just Norm's overactive imagination, but it bothered me. And once again, my spidey senses kicked in, and I began wondering what the hell Johnny was up to. He was probably cutting some side deal on something, the way he had been doing all his life. And he had every right to do so as long as it didn't impact our casino operations. But it still bugged me. It shouldn't, but it did. And Danny's words came to mind: "There's nothing better than visceral analysis."

Chapter Eighteen

I'm just a soul whose intentions are good,
oh Lord please don't let me be misunderstood.
—Song Lyrics….The Animals

Everything was coming up roses, or so we thought. Rylee was doing great at preschool. Debbie was thrilled with her pregnancy, and at five months, she had just received a glowing medical report from the doctor. On the business side, the casino management and dealer school was nicely under way, and we were beginning to replace the old guard at the other Diamond Resorts operations. I was confident that there would soon be a discernable improvement in casino profits throughout the system.

Unfortunately, while everything seemed to be coming together elsewhere, including our King's Own Resort, Debbie got herself embroiled in a big problem on the home front. One day when she was dropping Rylee off at the Mary Star of the Sea preschool, she noticed Maria Diego's car pulling up behind her to let Joanie out. Debbie waved, and when she received a rather tepid response, she got out of her car and walked back to Maria's.

Debbie was stunned when she saw her.

Maria had two black eyes, and her nose was swollen across her face.

"Maria, what happened to you?" gasped Debbie, and that was all it took for a torrent of tears to take hold of Maria.

Debbie said, "Let's go somewhere where we can talk."

Maria looked at Debbie with panic in her eyes.

"No!" she said. "I have to go." While Debbie watched helplessly, Maria sped off.

Throughout dinner that night, both Marilyn and I noticed that something was bothering Debbie. She refused to talk about it until after Rylee had been put to bed. Once our little girl was asleep, we took our coffee cups into the living room, where she shared the disturbing story with us.

"Chance, I don't know what to do!" wailed Debbie.

I said, "I honestly don't know, either. But whatever you do, you have to be careful. That Raymundo's a cokehead, and he's got a lot of firepower."

"Debbie," Marilyn said, "Chance is right. Sometimes the best thing to do is to do nothing. Time is a great healer. And if it happens again, she should go to the police. Let them handle it."

Two days later, Debbie got a call from Maria. "Debbie, Debbie, I'm so scared. So scared. I'm at the Mega Mart. He only let me out to buy groceries. I'm using another shopper's phone. Can you come now? Come quick!"

"I'll be there in ten minutes." Debbie raced to the supermarket and bounded through the doors, looking left and right. Standing at the end of an aisle, near the dairy items, stood Maria. She wore large sunglasses and long sleeves. The sunglasses didn't quite cover the black and blue bruises on her face.

She stepped back from Debbie's embrace. "Don't touch me," she said in a hoarse whisper. "Stay away. I don't know what to do." She began to cry. "He'll kill me if they see us talking. Get another phone for me. He has smashed every phone in the house."

Debbie said, "Take mine. You can call me on Chance's phone."

Maria took the phone and turned away. "I have to go," she said.

The next morning, my phone rang. I answered and heard Maria's faint voice asking for Debbie. A minute later, when Debbie disconnected, she told me about their conversation.

"I can only talk for a few minutes," Maria had said. "Raymundo's crazy. I'm so scared. I don't know what I'm going to do. I've got to get away from here."

"What happened?"

"Raymundo found out about me and Marco."

Debbie asked, "What do you mean?"

"Marco and me...we...we been loving." Maria was crying harder. "I love him. He was going to take me away. He was going to rescue me." Now she was sobbing loudly. "I think Raymundo killed him!"

"Killed him...?" a stunned Debbie said. "But you and Marco? You and Marco..? When? How?"

"Raymundo would do anything. *Anything!*" Maria interrupted. And with that, Maria was off the line.

Debbie's face had drained of blood. She relayed the conversation and then said, "Chance, what am I going to do?"

"First, she has to get away from him. She and Joanie. After that comes the problem of keeping them hidden and alive."

"She said that she thought Marco was probably dead. Do you think Greg could arrest Raymundo?"

"Where's the evidence? Greg can't arrest him just on Maria's suspicions."

Maria didn't call back the next day, or the day after. On the third day, Debbie finally received the call she was so desperately waiting for. As soon as Debbie heard Maria's voice, she said, "Will Raymundo let you go to church?"

"Probably. Maybe. Yes, I think."

"Good. Will he let Joanie go too?"

145

"Yes."

"Good, OK, I think I've got an idea that might work, but it's Thursday now, and there isn't enough time to put everything together for *this* Sunday, so I want you and Joanie to go to church as normal. Here's the plan."

Debbie then laid out her idea and quickly received Maria's worried agreement that it just might work.

"OK, think about it, and call me on Monday."

"Thanks, Debbie, I will." The line went dead.

That night we called Toronto. "Father Anthony, how would you like a quick trip to Balboa? We've got a big problem, and we sure could use your help," I said.

Sunday came and went, and Debbie got her call from Maria. "Yes, I think your idea will work. Raymundo will let me and Joanie go to church, but he sends us with a driver who watches over us. And I'm afraid about Father Diego. He won't help."

"That's OK," said Debbie. "Don't worry. Thanks to our friend Father Anthony, the archdiocese has asked Father Diego to go to Tampa for meetings. He won't be around."

A week later, everything was in place. A car was positioned in the church parking lot, and a Cessna 150 was standing by for the short hop to Treasure Cay on Abaco Island in the neighboring Bahamas.

Maria arrived at the church about fifteen minutes early. After dropping Joanie at the children's Bible study in the rectory, she took a seat in the front row. Debbie arrived a few minutes later and took her seat on a side aisle near the rear of the church, close to the rectory door.

Father Anthony, the guest priest from Toronto, gave a wonderful sermon, culminating with the request that all in attendance join him for communion. He blessed the wine and asked that those present come forth to share the experience with him in God's house. He did so with an impassioned zeal seldom seen at Mary Star of the Sea Church. As a result of his passion, almost the entire congregation crowded as one to the front. Maria moved quickly to be the first to take communion, and as she did, Debbie slipped out the rectory door and gathered up Joanie, who was so happy to see Mommy's friend. Together they dashed out the rear exit and met Maria, who had quickly left the altar and bolted out the side door.

Raymundo's driver was trapped. Surrounded by the congregation all trying to take communion at the front, he did his best to elbow his way to the exit. Unfortunately for him, by the time he got outside, all he could do was watch hopelessly as Maria and Joanie's car raced down the driveway to Sunset Boulevard, which led directly to the airport.

But as their car approached the exit, a black Cadillac pulled across the roadway, blocking their path. Trapped. Those leaving church were now pulling up behind, and there was absolutely nowhere for them to go. Paranoia has its place. Raymundo had instructed his guys to be safe, not sorry. He had anticipated just such an escape attempt and had a second car positioned to block the exit just in case.

Terrified, Maria choked back her scream as the Caddy door opened and one of Raymundo's goons walked back to the escape car. No rush, no fuss, he just tapped on the window, and when she lowered it, he quietly asked Maria and Joanie to please come with him. He said he would take them home now.

Completely devastated, Maria could do nothing but comply meekly.

Does your life ever return to normal after you've orchestrated a failed escape attempt? The next forty-eight hours were the longest

147

of Debbie's life. She was as hurt by the experience as Maria—the only difference was that she didn't have the scars to prove it. It was a few days before Maria made contact with Debbie.

"Thank God you've called," said Debbie. "I've been worried sick. I could only have stayed away from your home for about one more day, and then I would have had to go and see Raymundo. What happened?"

"It wasn't too bad," Maria said. "Raymundo only knocked me down once. I think he was proud that he had caught me. He showed me how smart he was. But he said it was the last time he would let me get away with trying to escape. The guards are really scared, too. They know that if I escape when they are supposed to be watching me, Raymundo would probably kill them too. What should I do? This is almost worse than being dead…"

"Oh Maria," Debbie said, "it's awful, I know. But at least you and Joanie are OK. Now we just have to figure out a new plan. In the meantime, you stay safe, be well, and call me when you can."

"OK, I will. But Debbie…"

"Yes?"

"He knows about you. I didn't say nothing. He tried to get me to say that you were helping me to get off the island, but I said nothing. But he knows. He said so. He said that both his driver and Joanie told him that you took her out of the church. So for sure he knows. He says you better watch out."

Debbie went cold all over.

Chapter Nineteen

For every action there is an equal and opposite reaction.
—Sir Isaac Newton

There was only a short time until the casino opened, and plenty remained to be done. Everything had to be ready for our soft opening on October 15. With so many newly trained staff, we thought it best to open on a limited basis, giving ourselves the opportunity to closely monitor and coach our personnel in preparation for the grand opening on November 29. Typically, September through mid-December, which coincides with the most active part of the hurricane season, is the slowest part of the year. We figured it would give operations a chance to ramp up their systems before Christmas, when we hoped all hell would break loose and we would be swamped with business.

I would have liked to have been able to focus solely on the King's Own opening, but I was also very involved in the investigations and re-staffing of the casinos at the other Diamond Resorts as well. However because all my prior businesses had always operated on a *next man up* basis, my seasoned senior execs from Toronto were extremely valuable in this regard and could step into virtually any situation with relative ease. Very quickly it became evident that we were managing our way to better performances across the board. I had appointed Barry Denton Executive VP of casino operations, responsible for heading the mission. He had responded to the challenge with great vigor. It was a matter of *right guy* at the *right place*. But he did something once appointed that impressed me the most. He asked if I would offer Johnny the identical position of Executive VP as well. When explaining his request, he reiterated that the challenges we faced were many, and as matters stood, DR's money was being siphoned off every hour that corrective measures weren't implemented.

He said, "Quite frankly, Johnny is one of the most capable gaming executives in the western hemisphere. And we need that caliber of management, front line, as soon as possible." When I raised my usual cautionary concerns about Johnny, Barry immediately cut me off. "Right now I'd rather have Johnny on our side. Just make sure that his employment contract contemplates only reasonable termination notice. And make sure that he doesn't have the ability to sue us for wrongful dismissal, because if my instincts are right, he'll be gone in six months. But right now I need him. And you can be confident that I won't place him in a position where he can contaminate the incoming management and staff."

I've often wished I could have cloned Barry.

As Mom used to say, *"It never rains, but it pours."* To complicate matters further, Goldberg called and told me that within a week or so I could expect a visit from a consortium that was considering buying the golf courses and maybe the casino and hotel operation as well.

My remarks in the New York boardroom hadn't fallen on deaf ears. Following my departure, there were some board members who decided that they didn't like the idea that their corporation was being ripped off. They remained highly skeptical that my team and I could right the listing casino ship and had directed Findlay to explore the feasibility of selling off the casino operations. Of course, that was their prerogative, but I remained equally positive that given only a little time, we could weed out the bad apples throughout the system and install honest, professional casino management and staff.

It was only a day later that I received a call advising me that a delegation of potential purchasers, would arrive on our doorstep only a few days before our grand opening. I immediately got in touch with Bill Goldberg, hoping to get a handle on just who these people were and what their background was. Even though I had limited big-business experience, I knew it was always wise to know your buyer and their motivations. Bill hadn't provided much background on them but I wasn't too surprised when they turned out to be from Mexico. And I was even less surprised when my instincts were borne out and that most likely they represented the drug cartel headed by *El Chapo* (Shorty) Guzman.

It was common knowledge that the drug cartels were making a concerted effort to put their huge cash flows to work in legitimate businesses. This was primarily the result of the pressure being applied by the American DEA and more recently Homeland Security, with both agencies seeking to stem the flow of dirty funds being deposited in banks. The United States had recently demanded that banks worldwide adhere to and enforce the "Know Your Customer" rule. If a country allowed capital to circulate through their institutions that was subsequently found to have been generated by illegal means, both the offending bank and the country as a whole could be subjected to severe embargoes. As a result of this increased scrutiny, the drug cartels were finding it difficult to hide or even utilize their vast profits. One tried-and-true method (and by far the most effective) was to launder their cash by buying into legitimate businesses. Hence the attraction of acquiring select properties and operations from the Diamond Resorts portfolio.

Upon their arrival and after introductions were made all around, I quickly realized that these guys hadn't just fallen off a turnip truck. The cartel representatives were sharp. They were savvy. And they brought with them both an accountant *and* a lawyer, who happened to be one of the 99 percent that gave all the other lawyers a bad name. He was an absolute know-it-all, sullen-faced jerk. But now we knew two things: they were serious, and they had conveyed a sense of urgency.

Chairman Findlay had seen to it that the prospects were provided with considerable material, much of which had been gleaned from the information my team had originally compiled, and which I had "sold" to Diamond Resorts by virtue of our blackjack game. But the cartel had done their own due diligence and knew our business inside out—they weren't here to waste anyone's time. And while I had no problem providing quality answers to their probing, I still couldn't help but wonder how they knew so much about our internal workings and our Achilles heels, such as the theft we were experiencing at some of our other casinos. Surely that information wouldn't have been provided by Findlay or Goldberg.

They did the dance well and although they feigned an interest in the golf courses and the hotel, it was obvious that their primary interest was the casino. They were smooth too, and quick to compliment us on the casino's general feel and theme, which we had so painstakingly created months ago. After much analysis, we had decided to lever up on the royalty theme. After all, the resort was called the King's Own. Our mottos were, "Let us treat you like Royalty" and "Come play with us. You'll get more than your money's worth." They knew how proud we were of our operation, and even though we knew they were stroking us, it still made us feel good.

The cartel guys also really liked the idea that we were holding a World Series of Poker event at our card room in conjunction with the casino grand opening. It was gratifying to learn that even in Mexico they had seen our promotion for the poker tournament. And I was particularly pleased when they commented on our promise that regardless of the number of entrants, we were going to provide $25,000 more in prize money than we would take in from entry fees. This was unheard of in the poker-tournament world, where most hotels and casinos automatically took 35 percent of the entry fees as their profit. Players in the poker world loved that we were putting more money into the prize pool than we were taking out. But I knew that even though we were sacrificing profits short term, that the resulting publicity would definitely benefit our operations well into the future.

They also knew all about our Caribbean Shoot-Out Golf tournament that was to be held the week following the Poker Tournament.

All in all, the prospective buyers indicated they were suitably impressed, and one of them even said he was going to come back to play in the golf tournament. He even tried to get comped for the $5,000 entry fee. The cheap prick. Here he was representing an organization that took in hundreds of millions of dollars each year, and he was trying us on for $5,000. I just told him, "Sorry, it's against corporate policy. If we comp you, then we'll have to comp Raymundo. And if we comp Raymundo, then we'll have to comp all the DEA agents who are here tailing you guys." He laughed and laughed. We did comp all their rooms, though. That relatively small courtesy only made good business sense, and as Dad always said *"Better safe than sorry"*.

My part of the dog and pony show only took a couple of hours. Once I had provided them with my perspective from 10,000 feet, I turned the guys over to JoAnn for resort specifics. She was delighted to show them around her pride and joy, which included the hotel, the rooms, and the back of the house for the restaurants, bars, and convention facilities. I also asked Johnny and Norm to conduct the balance of the tour, including the pools, beach amenities, golf courses, and casino. I had just finished my instructions and was on my way back to my office, when I had a *Whiskey, Tango, Foxtrot* moment! It occurred to me that the only way they could be so well informed was if somebody was feeding them firsthand information. And who would have been the most likely candidate to try to back door us? If my instincts were right, it could only be on*e guy.*

Chapter Twenty

Hockey is a sport for white men.
Basketball is a sport for black men.
Golf is a sport for white men dressed like black pimps.
—Tiger Woods

I was headed to the golf course. We had managed to get eighteen of the thirty-six holes fully operational along with the driving-range facilities and the clubhouse. The Pete Dye design looked great, and I knew the round-the-clock effort it had taken to get it to this stage would pay off handsomely. Knowing that many poker-tournament players also played golf, I realized that this would be an incredible opportunity to showcase our golf-course amenities.

I was still more than a little cranky about our former greenskeeper. We would have had both courses open had it not been for him. But kudos to JoAnn and her accounting team. One of her staff had previously worked at another golf facility back in the states and as a result, had a visceral understanding of the cost of golf course equipment and the essential fertilizers and materials. Fortunately for us, he also knew that grass on our island grows like crazy.

In fact, the local joke was that if we threw grass seed on boulders, coral beach sand, or sidewalks, and gave them enough water, a person would have to get the hell out of the way or they'd be lost in a jungle. It wasn't far from the truth. I thought that we would have to sod the areas that had been washed out by the hurricanes in 2004, but no. All our guys had to do was recontour the fairways a bit, reinstall the irrigation system, sprinkle some grass seed, and presto...in two weeks we had meaningful grass. And in four weeks we had lush fairways and perfect greens.

It was all good news for us, but for our greenskeeper, not so much. Our accountant had taken one look at the fertilizer bill and knew intuitively that the numbers were way off. He told us that we could have fertilized all of San Vida with the amount that had appeared on the invoice. A little investigation confirmed that the greenskeeper was writing out the POs for twice as much fertilizer as he needed. The shipment would arrive, and the invoice would match the PO and would be paid. Once that was done, he'd ship the excess material back to the supplier and have the refund check made out to him. It was an old scam, and all he needed was a confederate at the supplier end. And it would have worked if it wasn't for our eagle-eyed Boy Scout accountant.

Attracting the tournament to our facility was a major coup. Norm had heard rumors that the Great American Golf Shoot-Out was looking for a new home. For twenty-five years, the tournament had been held at the Miami Doral G&C, but the powers that be had tired of the event. It was obvious to us that by hosting the event, we would ensure repeat business from a huge number of participants who were big-time, if not legendary, gamblers, so we had put on a full court press. We would give all tournament players a 50 percent discount on their green fees and their hotel accommodations and we'd treat them like kings and queens. It was great PR.

There would be seventy-two male golfers for three days, and thirty-two women golfers for their own two-day event. For both tourneys, each foursome would be comprised of an A, B, C, and D player based on handicaps. The format was to be the team's best ball score, and the team would also get to deduct 25 percent of the captain's handicap. But therein lay our first major challenge.

Our registration materials had made it clear that we were going to verify *all* handicaps, but I guess a few of the players thought we were kidding. Believe me when I say that there was considerable consternation when some showed up for their practice round and were told they couldn't play until we spoke to someone at their home course. Luckily, I had a secret weapon: Debbie. She has wonderful people skills. Those whose handicaps hadn't been independently verified were turned over to her, and it was her responsibility to get the home course contact information for each golfer. She would then make a private and confidential phone call to their course, obtaining the proper verification. She did a great job. It was also double win for me, because not only did I have someone I could trust to handle this delicate situation, but it also gave Debbie something to do other than sitting around the house worrying and waiting for a call from Maria. By the time she was finished making her calls, and we had reset some of the handicaps as a result of her intel, there were really only three tournament player wannabes who ended up being problems. With two, we couldn't find anyone to provide the confirmation we needed. The third, according to his home course pro was, "just a no good, lying, son of a bitch."

Because I was the grand pooh-bah on the spot, I had to make the tough call, and while all three were gigantically pissed, I really had no choice. I offered two of them a deal: I would refund them their money in full *or* cut in half the handicap that they had provided and move them up two categories. So if they had said they were a C, they were now an A, and if they said they were a ten handicap, they were now a five. They were grumpy but agreed. But the last guy had the potential to be too problematic, so I personally gave him his money back and told him that we just couldn't bend the rules to accommodate him. I also gave him a new golf shirt and because he had travelled all the way to San Vida and wouldn't be able to play, I also comped his room for two nights. He still wasn't happy. But as my dad would have said, *"Fuck him, let's move on."* Dad always had a way with words.

While the due diligence we performed, by verifying handicaps, provoked a lot of controversy initially, we soon had the legit guys both congratulating us and thanking us for giving them a straight-up deal. Once again it confirmed my belief that if people are treated honestly and with respect, they will find ways to tell others of their positive experience. And that's the best advertising in the world.

We did a couple of other things that were unique to the tournament as well. We removed all the movable tee markers and made everybody play from the sunken plate tee markers. I knew that some of the reprobates in attendance would have no compunction about moving tee markers either back or to less desirable locations after they had hit their tee shots.

We also had pari-mutuel betting, and the players loved it. The total betting would have rivalled the daily handle at some of the C horse-race tracks up north. And characters—we had more than Disney World.

While conducting our handicap verifications, we had been warned time and again about some of the entrants. The best of the worst were the self-proclaimed *Pigs of the Caribbean.* This nefarious group was made up of eight grifters, bail bondsmen, bookmakers and professional gamblers. I also got to know a guy who was as out of place as a black preacher at a Ku Klux Klan rally. He said he was a dress manufacturer of all things. During the run-up to the tournament we had a coffee together. Jimmy Dunn was an unforgettable guy with a joke or a humorous story for every occasion. At our first meeting he told me that he wasn't actually a dress manufacturer. He said he was really a distributor. He told me that he makes a lot of money selling dresses, then he distributes it to his wife, his kids and his two girlfriends.

Although I had no intention of trying to stay up with our guests in the drinking Olympics, I nevertheless had a great time at our cocktail party the night of the practice round. Their stories and exploits would have made a hell of a movie. I sat with Jimmy Dunn, and once again he was a hoot, with more stories than Bayer has aspirins.

He told me that he had learned about the tournament from the Pigs of the Caribbean. He had met some of them at a poker tournament in Las Vegas and they had convinced him to come over to Balboa. The only problem with dressmaker Jimmy was that he drank too much. He ended up falling asleep at our table, which kind of put a damper on things for me. I've always been uncomfortable around people who drank to excess and I could tell that this guy was a bit of a lush. I didn't say anything, but I knew he was ripe for the picking, particularly with these pirates around.

The tournament was a tremendous success, and the decision to carefully scrutinize and verify all the handicaps of the participants was applauded and commented on by virtually everybody. The pretournament welcome party had set a positive vibe. Our golf pro, J. B. Kemp, acted as master of ceremonies and had kicked things off by welcoming everyone and by providing results from a survey that had ostensibly been conducted during the previous year's tournament. She said that one of the most interesting results from the survey was that 86 percent of the players from the previous year's tournament said that they had had sex in the shower that year. The other 14 percent said they hadn't, but it was only because unlike the other 86 percent, they hadn't been in prison that year.

JB also took a few minutes to remind everyone of the rules for a Scramble event, for example - mandatory minimum three drives per player and after the drives everyone had to play their next shot one foot from the selected ball position. She finished by asking all assembled to ponder one of golf's greatest dilemmas. She asked a *"What would you do?"* question.

She said, "on the eighteenth hole, your playing partner hits his ball into the woods and just as you find it and slip it into your pocket, he yells that he has found his ball and that he has an open shot to the green. The guy then hits his ball up six feet from the hole. Now the question is, *Do you, or don't you, call him a lying, cheating no good SOB?*

Good stories, great laughs.

However, the day after the tourney I was reminded that professional gamblers share a unique character trait: *none of them have a conscience.*

Most civilians think of professional gamblers as romantic figures sitting at a poker table, making a living playing cards in exotic locales or hanging out at a race track drinking highballs and smoking cigars. That's a long way from the truth. Most grind out a buck by playing what they play best, which is known in the vernacular as their *road game.* They could be pool players, golfers, bridge players or even chess, checkers, or backgammon players. And, for the most part, they can make an OK living. At least until they hook a *live one.* Their target could be a mullet who didn't know he was outclassed. Or it could be a player with an outsize ego or a boozehound or druggie who couldn't comprehend their vulnerability. But when their target goes on *tilt,* that's when the professionals make their move and go for the jugular. That's when the pros make their big score.

After a bad beat or an extra drink or when something upsetting occurs, some people lose that little bit of control or discipline that is so necessary for survival when gambling. When control goes out the window and ego takes over, the mark will begin to plunge. When that happens, it's all over. Like when Willie Nelson took on Amarillo Slim and lost $250,000 playing backgammon. Willie said he thought they were just having a friendly game. And they were, until he went on tilt and began to chase his losses.

A few bad breaks and all of a sudden the mark loses control. And once under water, there's no chance of climbing out. On tilt, it seems they can't do a thing right. They get snake bit, and lady luck all but disappears. And to add insult to injury, when they lose their composure, they simply don't know how or when to quit. I've seen it happen too often. And being in the gambling industry I'll see it again and again. That's exactly what happened the day after our golf tournament.

The Pigs of the Caribbean had booked two tee times for the following day and had set up their own eight-man, eighteen-hole tournament. On the surface everything looked OK, but J. B. became aware of a situation that she thought warranted my attention. She called and asked if I could come over to the course. When I arrived she told me that it looked like the Pigs had hooked a supremely intoxicated whale. Jimmy Dunn was in the crosshairs. This was the same dressmaker who had fallen asleep at our table.

Before the tournament, I had asked our staff to keep their eyes and ears open for any issue that might affect the reputation of our golf tournament or our resort, so J. B. was doing exactly as I had asked.

According to J. B., Jimmy and a Pig named Reg Hammel had a side game going, starting at $10,000 a hole. A lot of coin to be sure, but as far as I was concerned, that amount wasn't anything a well-heeled player couldn't handle. However, there was more to the story. When the players came through the clubhouse after they had played their first nine holes, the foursome had ordered some drinks to go and then went into the can. As soon as they returned to their carts, our savvy bartender Tommy had told J. B. that something wasn't right. After Jimmy went into the washroom, Tommy was asked to change the drink orders, and make Jimmy's drinks both doubles and to make the drinks for the other players without booze. He also said that in addition to the mixed drinks, one of the other players bought six mini bottles of vodka. Tommy said it was pretty obvious to him that one guy was being set up and that he was soon going to be bombed out of his mind. Because of the doubled-up drinks, he'd never know what hit him.

I heard Tommy and J. B. out and began to tell them that while I appreciated their concern, this situation really wasn't any of our affair and that my personal policy is to live and let live. I mean everybody has to make a buck, and if the piranhas were taking down a guy who was stupid enough to put himself in that position, what were we to do? It wasn't our job to save the world.

But because they were so emotional about it, and because I had really enjoyed Jimmy's half-pissed company at the cocktail party, I finally relented and told them that with reluctance, I would grab a cart and look in on the situation.

I caught Jimmy's group on the tee box of the par-three fourteenth hole. There was another foursome already on the green ahead, so I had an opportunity to visit the guys while the other group was putting out. It was immediately apparent that poor old Jimmy was three sheets to the wind. He knew he was on planet earth but had no idea in what hemisphere.

"Hey, Jimmy, how you doing, man?" I asked.

"Not so good. These guys are beating me like a drum. I'm down sixty."

"Sixty? Sixty what? Sixty dollars?"

"Sixty grand."

I turned to Reg, who tried to laugh it off. He shrugged and said, "He's not having the best day. Seems he can't catch a break."

"Is that right?" I asked. "And in the process you're going to carve him a new asshole, aren't you Reg? I know you're on a roll here, but poor Jimmy looks like he has been ridden hard and put away wet. Why don't you give him a break and let him finish the game tomorrow when he's not under the weather?"

"WHO ARE YOU?" stormed a belligerent Jimmy Dunn. "Get outta my kitchen! I been playin' golf and gambling since you was in short pants, so don't you be messing with my game. I'm down sixty grand now! And you want me to quit while I'm down sixty grand? Who are you anyway? We gonna step it up right now to fifty grand a hole. Ain't that right, Reg?"

"Yeah, I guess so." Reg shrugged. "But that's a ton of money, Jimmy. You sure you want to play for that much?"

"You're damn right, you sorry ass mother...We gotta GAME!"

"You hear that, mister high and mighty?" Jimmy yelled as he got right in my face and backed me up across the tee box.

The group ahead had finished putting out but were looking back at the commotion on our tee box, when all of a sudden

Jimmy grabbed his ball and tee and even though they hadn't cleared the green, took a mighty swing and plopped his ball in the water hazard.

"There," he said accusingly. "You satisfied now? You satisfied? Did you come all the way out here just to bug me while I've got a big game going? Well if that's your idea, it's working. Now leave me alone!"

Man, I couldn't believe this was the same funny, life of the party Jimmy. I thought to myself if that's what booze does to a person, why would they ever drink? I couldn't say anything while the other guys were teeing off, but as everybody was walking back to their carts, I took one last shot.

"Jimmy, we want you to have a great time here at King's Own, and we want you to come back here again. But that just ain't going to happen if you lose a hundred grand today. Why don't we just pack it in and you and I can maybe take them on in a match tomorrow?"

He looked at me for a moment, and I thought he was considering the wisdom of my idea, when all of a sudden he exploded. He started yelling at me even louder this time. I thought he might even hit me as again, he got right in my face.

His boozy breath was just awful, and as I kept backing up off the tee box, and away from the guys, he just kept walking toward me and yelled one last time, "Now you get OUTTA my kitchen! We got a fifty-grand-a-hole bet, and I'm taking these candy asses *down*." And then with his back to the other players, he looked right into my eyes and *winked*...and then he *smiled!* Then he winked again, turned, and stumbled back to the others and said, "OK, youse mothers I'm loaded, and I'm hunting for bear."

I damn near fell down in shock. I realized that I was seeing the acting performance of a lifetime. This guy was better than Al

164

Pacino. It was all I could do to collect myself, make my apologies, put my tail between my legs, and retreat back to the clubhouse.

On my way back, I passed a number of other golfers, all of who must have thought I was a loony tune. I was laughing out loud and pounding the steering wheel in absolute delight. The entire episode that I had just witnessed, was a complete charade.

As much as I was anxious to learn the outcome, I couldn't stick around. I had to get back to the casino. So I asked our J.B. to go out to their foursome when she thought they'd be on about the seventeenth hole to watch and report how the events shook out.

I didn't let on even a hint of my suspicions—to her or to anyone else. But I did ask her to come to my office at the casino once she knew the outcome. When she showed up a few hours later, I took great delight in asking Sy, who was playing Hold'em, and Norm, Johnny, and Barry to join me in our mini boardroom. They all wondered what was up and probably feared the worst, as I wasn't in the habit of calling snap meetings unless there was a problem.

I opened the conversation by saying, "Guys, you all know J. B. Kemp, our golf pro. She has some golf results to share with us, and even though I don't know the outcome, I thought you'd like to hear the story." I then related how I had met and enjoyed this jovial boozehound from Chicago at the golf tournament and how the Pigs of the Caribbean had set a trap to take him down earlier in the day. I also described what happened when I went out to the Fourteenth hole to try to save his sorry ass.

I've never met a golf pro yet who wasn't a bit of a raconteur. And J.B. didn't let me down. She relished bringing us up to date.

"Well, as Chance told you, Jimmy dunked his tee shot on Fourteen. He re-teed from the forward drop area, muscled it up to the hole and two-putted for a five. Reg three-putted for a four, so at that point, Jimmy was down one hundred and ten thousand dollars."

Even our tight little group, accustomed to big games as they were, murmured their concerns and dismay for poor Jimmy. Sy, who rarely comments on anybody, simply said, "The stupid fuck."

"So they played fifteen, both bogeyed and tied the hole, which must have seemed like a major league victory for Jimmy, if he could even understand what was going on. He appeared pretty wobbly but did agree to a carryover on sixteen. So at this point, they are playing for a hundred grand per hole. Beaucoup bucks. Now keep in mind that this is their fourth golf game in four days, and at this point, neither player had shown enough talent to hit their way out of a wet paper bag. Best case, they were usually tagging their drives around two hundred yards. On sixteen, they both hit good drives, and both hit their second shots short of the green. Reg chipped to about five feet and missed the putt. Jimmy weaved up to his ball and chipped to two feet and made his putt. The guy who was describing the action to me said at that point he thought he heard Reg's asshole slam shut. He called it rigor mortis of the sphincter muscle.

"So on the seventeenth tee box, Jimmy was down only ten thousand dollars, but Jimmy said he was having so much fun that he wanted to keep on playing for a hundred thousand a hole and asked if somebody would please get him another beer. On seventeen, Reg hit first and dubbed his drive about one hundred fifty yards. Then believe it or not, Jimmy did the same. Then they pooched their second shot another twenty-five yards. They both had about one thirty-five to the hole. Reg hit it to thirty-five feet, Jimmy to six feet. Reg two-putted and a gleeful semi-stoned Jimmy made his first putt of the day. So at that point, Jimmy was up ninety thousand.

"The last hole was anticlimactic. Playing for a hundred grand, Reg reached back and nailed his drive about two hundred twenty yards, which was about twenty yards farther than he had hit a ball all day. And old roly-poly, semi-drunk Jimmy sailed his ball *over* Reg's by another ten yards. Reg was done like dinner. He just didn't know it yet. He tried to get that extra twenty yards out of his fairway wood but, instead, hit a *Mickey Mantle: a dead yank.* One hundred fifty yards hard left. Long story short, Reg dumped his long iron into the sand trap to the right of the green, blasted out, and two-putted for a bogey six. Jimmy almost made the green in *two!* Then he chipped to five feet and two-putted for a par and picked up $190,000 for his day's work.

"Thanks J.B." I smiled. "Guys, we have just had the privilege to witness one of the best hustles, and one of the best acting jobs ever. It was a big-time win for a player who was in the crosshairs to be scammed. Instead, he turned the tables and scammed the scammers. It was an amazing performance. The end result kind of warms the cockles of my heart."

Chapter Twenty-One

The more things change, the more they stay the same.
—Anonymous

"Chance, we need to talk." I absolutely hated it when Norm started a conversation like that. He had waited until the room had cleared after J. B.'s story and then, once we were alone, launched into something that made my stomach lurch.

"Chance, I've got a bad feeling about those cartel guys, and I can't help but think that Johnny's somehow involved."

"What are you talking about?"

"Well, there's nothing that I can put my finger on for sure. But while Johnny and I were conducting the fifty-cent tour, there was just a little too much familiarity between him and them. Nothing overt. Nothing that I can point to. But while they wanted to check everything out personally, it was Johnny who was making sure they saw the one thing that they had really come to see—the count room. We only spent an hour and a half touring the sticks and bricks of the resort but spent a full two hours just delving into the count-room operations and the flow of cash from the slots, blackjack, Craps tables, and the other table games.

"Once the cartel guys and the lawyer got inside the count room, Johnny was in his element. He might as well have produced a *how-to video*, because we sure don't have any more secrets relative to the win percentages or cash flows in and out of this casino."

Playing the devil's advocate, I said, "Don't you think their questions were reasonable? I mean, after all, if they're conducting their due diligence, surely they're entitled to understand every aspect and nuance."

"Yeah I know," said Norm. "And I know you're right. But it wasn't just what Johnny was telling them…it was like he was confirming things he had already told them."

"What do you think's behind it?"

"I dunno. But Chance, I just know that somehow, someway, Johnny is hooked up with those guys. And do you remember a few weeks ago when I told you that I had seen Johnny at the Tropicana sitting with some Latinos?"

"Yeah."

"Well, I can't be sure, because I only kind of glanced at them, but I think one of the guys who took the count-room tour might have been at the Trop."

"OK, Norm. Don't ignore your intuition. I know you don't throw accusations around easily. But it's a lot to digest, so leave it with me to consider. I'll get back to you tomorrow."

When Norm left, I realized I had quite a dilemma. If he was right, I probably had a fiduciary duty to tell Goldberg ASAP. But tell him what? Tell him that my right-hand guy *thought* my left-hand guy was telling stories out of school? And if that was the case, why was he doing it?

That night while I slept I let my subconscious mull over the ramifications of what Norm had told me, and in the morning I realized that I had to act, even though it was based more on speculation than fact. I was just about to phone Goldberg, when Norm called and said, "Chance, we need to talk. Privately."

I was hating that expression more and more.

"Sure, Norm. When do you want to get together?"

"How about your place about six tonight? Barry will be with me."

I decided to put off my call to Goldberg, at least until I heard the guys out.

They arrived right on time and within twenty minutes, had me convinced that we had a problem. I also realized that if they were right, they might have uncovered a plan for a money-laundering scam that in scope, rivaled the one that Mafia bagmen used in the sixties and seventies. Back then the Las Vegas count rooms were off-limits, except to only the most trusted casino executives. When the incoming cash from the casino floor was counted, nothing was recorded until suitcases were filled each week. Those suitcases were then given to couriers who delivered millions of dollars of this unreported cash back to the mob owners and bosses in Chicago, New York, and Kansas City, totally undetected and out of the eyes of the Internal Revenue Service.

Barry Denton, like Norm and Johnny, had been a buddy of mine since forever. If Norm was second-in-command, certainly Barry was at least my number three. He could always be counted on, regardless of the situation. Originally, when we thought we were buying the King's Own, he had spent weeks working alongside Johnny, conducting our due diligence. As part of that process, he had visited all eight of the Diamond Resorts casinos scattered around the Caribbean and was the one who identified many of the scams that were being perpetrated by casino management and staff.

He had worked with me, and for me, ever since our school days back in Toronto—and if truth be told—he was the one who came up with the idea for us to start our lottery in high school. Even then, he showed an amazing aptitude for numbers, and he became by default, our designated bean counter. We always said that if you look up the word "accountant" in the dictionary, you would probably see a picture of Barry. And consistent with an accountant's demeanor, he was neat, quiet, and for the most part almost invisible. But when he did speak, his comments or ideas spoke volumes.

After hearing the guys out, I called Bill Goldberg at his home. After a very brief intro, I told him that while he was my direct report, in this instance all three of us needed to meet Chairman Findlay as soon as practically possible.

The next day at 10:00 a.m., Barry and I were on a plane to New York.

At 5:30 p.m. we met in the corporate boardroom, and after very terse greetings, I began. "Gentlemen, we have a problem of international scope—maybe one that could have serious ramifications for Diamond Resorts International. Several months ago, I sat in this very boardroom and told you and the board of directors that theft was rampant in your casinos. I'm pleased to advise that we have made tremendous progress in eradicating the culture of theft and pilfering. Give us two more months of operating results, and you will be astonished at the casino's improved performance. That's the good news. The bad news is that we think the stock of Diamond Resorts is being targeted as a takeover candidate, which in and of itself is not a bad thing, but we think the dynamics are much more troublesome and may have serious repercussions. And it's possible…"

The following morning at nine, we reconvened in the boardroom but this time with the full board in attendance.

Following brief opening remarks from Chairman Findlay, I began. "Mr. Chairman and gentlemen, our executive vice president with me today, Barry Denton, has been working twenty-four seven over the last few months to weed out those within your casino operations who have been stealing from Diamond Resorts and its guests. He has accomplished great things, which will become increasingly evident as the monthly reports from operations become available. Should there be questions, we will be available to respond to them at the conclusion of our remarks.

"But that is not why we are here. We are here with an unsubstantiated theory. But the magnitude, and potential for legal and Security and Exchange Commission problems is so acute that we, and Chairman Findlay believed you needed to be apprised of the situation immediately.

"We have reason to believe that money laundering is at the root of the current purchase overtures being made by the Mexican group. And we further believe that the listing of Diamond Resorts International stock on the New York Stock Exchange could be in jeopardy."

There were some audible gasps all around the table as Barry explained the hypothesis, "Although it is quite outside the scope of our casino investigations, I couldn't help but be intrigued by the performance of the Diamond Resorts stock and its run-up over the last six months. I've noted that it has moved from about eight dollars to over thirty dollars. If the matter wasn't so serious, I would make a joke here about the fact that the increase in the stock price has nicely coincided with the arrival of Chance Daly and his team. But unfortunately, that may be at least partially true. And I'll come back to that in a few minutes.

"We believe the Mexican drug cartel wants to control your casinos so they can comingle their ill-gotten cash with that of the DR casinos. Once they buy or control the casino operations, they can inject their drug-generated funds into casino operations and have those funds recorded as casino revenue. Of course, this means that the correspondingly higher profits will attract some additional tax consequences, but as far as they are concerned, that's a small price to pay if they can create clean, laundered cash. Obviously this additional flow of cash will serve to enhance casino revenues, making the operations seem more profitable, and therefore will drive up their value. But before we get too far ahead of ourselves, we want you to know that this is *not* unprecedented. And they have a twist that we'll get to in a minute, but first, some background.

"Back in the seventies, the Mafia acquired a small Philippine gold-mining company that had a listing on the New York Stock Exchange. It was called Bendow Consolidated and was trading at about two dollars when they took control. Bendow then acquired the Bahamian casino operations that had been created by Meyer Lansky. Over a couple of years, the casino and resort profits went to the moon. The market loved the stock. It went to eighteen dollars just based on its apparent solid performance.

"But then Carter Chemical, another NYSE company, came along and in a well-published attempt to diversify, it announced that it had acquired the rights for a gaming and casino license for the country of Haiti. Very good news. The company and stock showed great promise. The stock market loved the idea and their stock went from eleven bucks to sixteen. Not a bad return in six months, but it stalled there. However, when Carter Consolidated announced they were doing a takeover of Bendow Consolidated and their Bahamian casino operations, the stocks of both companies *doubled*. A huge win for their shareholders. But hold onto your seat.

"The two companies soon amalgamated under a new listing called International Resorts. That stock came on the New York

Stock Exchange at twenty-five dollars and was oversubscribed. It quickly jumped to thirty-six. Can you guess what happened within a year? First, the Haitian dictator, Baby Doc Duvalier, announced that the agreement to provide a gaming and casino license to Carter Consolidated was not transferable, and therefore the agreement was rendered null and void. And so started the slow slide in the International Resorts stock price.

"The company fought the cancellation in the Hague World Court, but the magic was gone. The stock slowly ebbed out of favor. There were a couple of brief run-ups when a good rumor would hit the papers, but those good news bits were almost always followed by another negative rumor or innuendo. Then began a severe drop in casino profits from the Bahamian gaming operations. The stock eventually sank from a high of almost forty dollars to a low of about fifty cents. It was finally delisted.

"Having heard that story, you might immediately think, 'Why would the mob allow that to happen? If the stock went from forty dollars to essentially zero, their holdings would be wiped out also.' Well, subsequent investigations uncovered one of the greatest short-selling scams of all time. It was eventually determined that the Mob designates were the original owners of *all three companies*. Behind the scene, they issued themselves treasury stock that cost them virtually nothing. Then, with collusion from writers of investor magazines and periodicals, and the media, they managed to drive up the price of the stock in a relatively short time. And as the stock was going up, they *sold off* their holdings. Then in an all-time incredible coupe d'état, they *shorted* more International Resorts stock! That's right—they sold stock they didn't own once it got around thirty-eight dollars and above. They continued to promote the stock making it go higher and at the same time they shorted shares by borrowing shares they didn't have, and sold them into the rising market. They kept doing this until word seeped out, which, of course, caused the stock to plummet. And once it crashed, that circumstance enabled them to buy back all the shares they had shorted. By conservative estimates they made over half a billion dollars—that's billion with a *capital B*."

There was dead silence.

Eventually, one of the board members spoke for everyone in the room when he said, "Jesus Christ!"

It took a few minutes for everyone to digest what they had heard, but soon the questions started, and with a true accountant's penchant for providing boring details, Barry took them chapter and verse through how he and his team were identifying the casino scams and how he had put the pieces together. He even mentioned how, in an amazing coincidence, he had fielded an identical question from two casino managers, who were working in different casinos over a thousand miles apart. Apparently, when he was giving each of them their walking papers in their respective casinos, they both asked, "Does Pablo know about this?" But when he tried to query them, on who Pablo was they immediately clammed up. But fortunately for us, it was enough to set off alarm bells.

It had taken some real detective work, but eventually we learned that Pablo was the designated Mexican cartel guy, who either had a hand in or was directing and encouraging the thefts. It all made sense too. Obviously, the cartel wanted to buy the casinos at the lowest price possible. So if the casinos were underperforming, the acquisition price would be that much less and the seller that much more malleable.

"It has obviously taken us a while to cobble the pieces together, but once we did, we knew that we had to advise you as soon as possible. And in the interest of full, true and plain disclosure, I am sorry to say that we may have an executive in our ranks who is, if not pulling the strings, either complicit or somehow involved. It's a long story and may have personal history attached, but suffice to say we will be cutting him loose in the very near future. In the meantime, it's a case of keeping our friends close and our enemies closer. We want to extract as much information from him as we can before we let him go. Confidentially, his name is Johnny Andrews."

There were remarkably few questions about casino thefts as the board members processed what they had heard from us, but there was some intense conversation about the US government's interest in money laundering. As the board members were going down that road, I broke in, and in an effort to conclude our portion, "Mr. Findlay, as far as everyone back in Balboa is concerned, other than my wife, I'm over in Miami for some medical tests. So I'd really like us to catch the 210 flight back before questions are raised about where we are and what we're doing. We came up here because we wanted to share our findings in person as soon as we understood the ramifications. Having done that, we will of course, continue to provide all relevant information as developments unfold, and we are always at your service should you need us to come back to New York.

"In the meantime, Barry and I have nothing to add regarding how and when you inform the SEC of the casino thefts and the current overtures relative to the purchase of the resort and casino operations. But we can assure you that casino operations are on the right track. We have weeded out many of the theft perpetrators and are well on our way to dramatically improving both casino profits and just as importantly, the corporate culture regarding our guests. You have my assurance that on all fronts, the best is yet to come.

"However, whether they will rise sufficiently to offset the negative publicity that may result from the issues we have just shared is another matter. But Barry and I believe that if and when you decide to terminate negotiations relative to the sale of the casinos, the cartel will most likely retaliate by at least threatening to undermine and damage the stock price. And some of us, having exposed their plan, might very well be in some danger. But that comes with the territory and we'll remain vigilant."

Barry and I had less than two hours to get to La Guardia and preclear immigration, so we bolted out of the boardroom after saying our hasty good-byes. We grabbed our overnight bags, jumped on the elevator, hailed a cab, and headed for the airport. We were quiet, lost in thought, when Barry suddenly said, "I feel like we just painted a big bull's-eye on our backs."

Chapter Twenty-Two

We all know how gambling and golf work...peaks and valleys, peaks and valleys...The key is to back off a little when you're losing, but pound them when you're winning.
—Rick Sanderson, Calgary, Alberta

Raymundo entered the casino and was acting like a bigger asshole than usual. A person had to wonder what allows psychopaths like Raymundo to continue to strut around in public, acting the tough guy. He bumped into a cocktail waitress in his haste to get to the tables, eliciting a "Hey! *Excuse me!*" from the short but attractive black waitress. Her comment was a clear but understandable violation of everything we had tried to instill in the staff. Probably it was just as well that Raymundo either didn't hear or ignored the remark as he stomped toward the high-stake Hold'em area in the rear of the casino.

He approached a security guard who was casing the crowded tables. "Did they get a no-limit Hold'em game going tonight?" demanded Raymundo. As the guard nodded toward a table to his immediate left he said in a friendly manner. " They sure did. Are you thinking of playing?" "NO" Raymundo spat back in a voice half the casino could hear. "NO! I'm GOING to play poker. What I'm THINKING about is PUSSY!!" And he barged over to where a small crowd was gathered watching the action of the big money game.

Raymundo recognized only Greg as he pulled back a chair to Greg's left and said, "I'm feeling lucky tonight. Can I join you?"

Looking up, Greg's first thought was conflicted. It started with *Not you again, jerk off!* But that thought was immediately followed by, *This guy is a loser and losers always lose. So of course you're welcome, asshole.* With more enthusiasm than he felt, Greg replied, "Yeah, sure, Raymundo, great to see you. Take a seat." Moving up behind Raymundo, one of his loyal goons quickly dropped a stack of hundred-dollar bills in front of him.

"Give me one hundred thousand in chips."

"Changing one hundred thousand!" shouted the dealer. This attracted the pit boss, who glanced quickly at Raymundo and then nodded toward the dealer.

While the chips were being counted out and the money jammed down into the cash slot, news traveled quickly, and the crowd around the table swelled. A cocktail waitress appeared and placed a double scotch in front of Raymundo. "Good luck, Ray."

"Thanks, babe," Raymundo said as he peeled a twenty off his stack. "Keep 'em coming, doll." He stuffed the bill down her top.

"You keep winning, they'll keep coming," she said, giving him a look that indicated to everyone watching that in the past she might have given Raymundo more than just drinks.

Whenever a *whale* joins a game in progress, bets have a tendency to cool a bit while everyone adjusts to the new vibe. Raymundo caught some lucky hands early, but his over-the-top bets scared off most of the players. Turning to Greg, he remarked, "A little gun-shy, boys? Where's the action?" Greg responded with a shrug.

Greg had played a lot of cards with Raymundo over the last few years, so he was very aware of Raymundo's tells. Frantic chip shuffling confirmed that tonight Raymundo was one cranked-up junkie. As a result Greg knew that if he played his cards right, he stood a good chance of parlaying his previously sizeable (but now seemingly meager) $30,000 into a big win. He realized that he had to be patient and pick his spots, but deep down he knew Raymundo was ripe for the plucking.

About an hour later, a handful of new players had come into the game, lost their stake, and bailed. But while Raymundo continued to knock back double scotches, he was managing to hang in and hadn't lost much of his stack. Nature eventually took its course, and Raymundo left for the can. While he was gone, Greg had considered cashing out. He had managed to build his stash to about $90,000, which was a pretty good pay day any way you look at it. But just as he was about to get up, Raymundo returned to the table, and when he did, it was obvious that he had done a few lines during his break. The chip shuffling intensified, and his legs were twitching even more than before. Greg thought, *This guy's going down. He can't play in this condition. He's going to lose a ton tonight, and whose better than me to take his money?*

It was only a few hands later that Raymundo peeked at his cards, and concurrently Greg noticed that Raymundo's legs went still. The finger shuffling continued, but something had aroused Raymundo. Greg figured he'd drawn a pair of high-face cards, likely queens or kings. Greg had the button, and when Raymundo raised $5,000, Greg only called.

On the flop, the dealer dealt a king, seven, and an ace rainbow and still no leg movement. Looking slowly at his cards, Raymundo bet another $5,000. One player folded, and the remaining player called. Greg looked at his hands again, and after about a minute of staring directly at Raymundo, he said,

"I'll see your five grand and raise you another five." Raymundo called, and the other player folded. The turn card was a queen of hearts. Raymundo wasted no time.

"That's ten thousand dollars to you, Greg."

After a long, penetrating stare, Greg said "OK, I'll take that bet and raise you another ten grand" as he pushed a pile of chips into the pot.

Raymundo didn't think twice. Pushing all his chips into the pot, he calmly remarked, "So you think you've got me, huh? Well, here's another thirty grand, which you'll have to cough up." The crowd let out a collective gasp, but the dealer quickly intervened.

"I'm sorry, sir, but I don't think you have enough chips."

Greg decided to make his move. "That's OK, dealer, he's only short about ten thousand dollars. I'll take his marker." Allowing the suspense to build, the dealer waited half a minute, before turning over the river card. It was a two of hearts.

"A fucking deuce. I doubt that's going to help either of us," said Raymundo before checking.

Greg piled on the pressure. "All in." The dealer started counting Greg's chips, while Raymundo pondered his situation.

"Greg, your ass is grass. I'll call you. How much did you bet?"

The dealer calmly replied, "The amount is thirty-seven thousand five hundred dollars." The legs started their nervous jumping again, but Greg knew that this cokehead had lost any semblance of good judgment.

"Greg, I've got two Cigarette boats, and I can only drive one at a time. How about it? Give me fifty grand in credit for it. I paid a hundred and a quarter for one of them just six months ago. One hundred twenty-five thousand dollars, and all I need is the credit anyway."

"Is it in good shape?"

"Damn right! I baby those boats. But I'm not planning on losing her anyway."

Greg had him just where he wanted him. It took only a few minutes for a promissory note to be hand written, confirming the agreement. Once done, the dealer said, "Gentleman, show your cards."

Greg was right. Raymundo had three kings. As Raymundo turned around to gloat to his backslapping goon, Greg slow rolled his two pocket aces, giving him trips for the win. The crowd erupted, and all hell broke loose! An enraged Raymundo grabbed one of the chip trays off the side table and threw it at the dealer, calling him every name in the book. It hit him right above the eye, and instantly there was blood everywhere. As soon as Raymundo stood up, yelling at the dealer, his goon started to move in. Reacting on instinct, Greg kicked back his chair and grabbed the goon, who looked as if he was going to attack the dealer. One of the poker players, tried to cool out Raymundo. "Ray—hey, man, what are you doing! Whoa, settle down. Hey, Ray, take it easy. The dealer was only doing his job…no harm done," he said.

While he was trying to calm Raymundo, security rushed over and not knowing what had happened, they started asking ten questions at once adding to the confusion. Somebody grabbed a towel from the boxman's tower and threw it to the dealer, who looked as though he was a heavy favorite to have a heart attack if he didn't bleed to death first.

It took a couple of minutes to bring order to the chaos, and in the interim Greg had pushed the goon up against the wall and looked as though he was going to strangle him. It was only later that Greg told us that he didn't know what the guy might do and how much firepower he was carrying, so he neutralized him just in case.

Once the bodyguard was restrained, Greg quickly took control of the situation. "Raymundo, shut up and listen. There's no need for this. We're having a friendly game of poker, and just because you lost doesn't mean you can take it out on the dealer. He's making twenty bucks an hour and you're throwing chip trays in his face. He doesn't get paid to take that kind of crap. Now you and your tough guy buddy get the hell out of here. I'll call you later to arrange to pick up the boat." Raymundo was at a loss for words, so he turned and stormed off. His goon meekly followed in his wake.

Operating a casino meant that anything under the sun was likely to occur, and often did. This Raymundo incident was just one of a number of episodes that happened elsewhere in the casino that same night. It must have been a full moon. We had been doing great business: the slots were full, the table games were full, and it seemed like every blackjack table had a couple of people standing behind the players, waiting for a seat. We had decided that there would only be two Craps tables open, which in retrospect, was a mistake. With all the player wannabes, the casino could have kept twice that number of tables busy.

Right around the time of the Raymundo episode, there had been a couple of other problems, and the casino manager had called me at home just to give me a heads-up. I listened and quickly decided a short meeting in the morning was in order. I asked him to invite the Craps dealer, the roulette dealer, and Sean, the poker dealer whom Raymundo had attacked, to come in the next day one hour before their six o'clock shifts started. I also made a quick call to Norm, explained the situations, and asked him to have Ozzie and George attend and because there might be some legal ramifications, I suggested that we invite Greg as well.

I had been making a conscious effort to wean myself off the need to get involved in day-to-day operations. And, for the most part, it was working out pretty well. But with three situations occurring almost simultaneously, I was more curious than anything and wanted to hear more.

Everybody showed up on time. I had long ago instituted a couple of rules about meetings that were proving to be very effective. All attendees were expected to be inside the meeting room at the appointed time or they were locked out, and access was denied. Also, any cell phone that rang during the meeting cost the owner fifty dollars. The staff learned quickly and some the hard way. But meetings always started on time. This one did as well.

"Well guys, I guess it never rains, but it pours." I started. "Thanks for coming in early and by way of introduction, a particular welcome to our dealers Declan Paul, Kaleb Alexander, and Sean McGonigal. Let's start with Sean, who looks a little worse for wear. And Norm, can I ask you to make notes for the file?"

It took Sean about ten minutes to relate the events of the previous night, all of which were corroborated by Greg.

"OK, I don't know what we could have done differently, so all we can do is hope that Raymundo cools down and comes back as a player. If it was anybody else, I'd be inclined to bar him, but he's good, live action, so unless Sean or Greg feel otherwise, I don't want to do that. You guys OK with that?"

"Yeah."

"Yah, I know what you mean. He's good business, so I'm fine with him coming back and I'll heal." Sean smiled.

"Thanks, guys. And I think Greg has a little something for you." With everyone watching, Greg peeled off one thousand dollars in cash and handed it to the dealer.

"You deserve this. Not only should you not have to put up with Raymundo's behavior, but I'd been meaning to thank you for dealing me those three Aces."

Sean accepted the money enthusiastically and I said, "That's kind of you, Greg. Now Sean can buy himself another shirt." Everyone laughed in agreement. Sean looked pleased.

"OK, now let's hear from Kaleb. Kaleb, you were dealing Craps on right base around eleven last night, right?"

"Yes, I was. As everyone knows, it was a jam-up night. Some guy got on a roll and made about eight passes. My layout was full with chips and bets everywhere. I was doing nothing but keeping my eyes on the cloth with my head down and my ass up. The player immediately across from me and two left of the dealer was up about four thousand. So he had a couple of full racks of reds, greens and blacks, and even a few white chips for the cocktail waitresses and dealers. Like I said, it was jam-up, and there must have been twenty people pressing behind the players, trying to see what was going on, while waiting for a chance to take a spot at the table.

"The shooter was at the other end and he had just made a hard ten, so I had five *'don't come'* bets to pick up and about twenty winning pass line and field bets to pay. When I finally straightened up and was waiting for the shooter to roll the dice again, I vaguely noticed that the player across from me had disappeared. But there was a new guy standing in his same spot, using his chips. The new guy called a twenty-five dollar, craps-eleven bet, and a five-dollar tip bet on eleven for the dealers. Then he threw the chips to the stick man. The bet for the dealers was, of course, a good thing. Tips are always a good thing."

There were smiles all around.

"I called out the bet he had made for the dealers so that the other dealers knew we had a *George* making bets for us. The shooter rolled a big-time winner! An eleven, so you know it was pandemonium. I collected the *don'ts,* paid the line and the prop bets, and, of course, the dealer's win, and got ready for another come-out roll. I had just given the dealer's winning eighty-dollar tip to the box-man to be locked up, when this lady across from me started screaming. She went nuts! She had just made her way through the crowd to try to get behind the new player and was freaking out. It took everybody a fraction of a second to figure out what was happening, but when we did, we realized the first player, who had disappeared, had actually fallen to the floor, and the guy behind him had simply stepped over him and was playing the first guy's chips!"

"What about the guy on the floor?"

"There was nothing about him. He was just lying there. Security arrived pretty quick. They put him in a wheelchair and dropped a sheet over him."

"And then what happened?"

"Nothing happened. The stick man called a come-out roll, and we just started playing again. But I guess it was a bad vibe because the shooter, who had just made nine passes, proceeded to crap out twice and then threw a four and then immediately sevened out," said Kaleb.

"But what happened to the guy on the floor?"

"Like I said, nothing happened to him. They put a sheet over him and he was wheeled away because he was stone-cold dead."

"What happened to the four thousand in chips that he had in front of him?"

"Must have been bad luck for the guy who stepped over him, too. It took another hour or so, but eventually he lost it all."

"Well, thanks for your report Kaleb. But why don't you stick around, because there's more to come. We're not finished yet and you may find it interesting," I said. "From what I hear, it sounds like it was a little more than just another day at the office. But I'm pleased that everybody handled things OK, although I don't know if the guy who stepped in to take over the dead guy's chips should have been allowed to do so. But if you didn't see him do it, then I guess it was no harm, no foul. We're not going to second-guess anybody. And from the sound of it, sometimes no call is the best call. However, soon after the guy died at the Craps table, we had another issue, this time on the roulette table. Declan, please tell us what happened."

"Yes, sir. Well, like in the rest of the casino, we were really busy. We had eight colors on the layout, so we had eight players each making a bunch of bets. There were so many chips out you could hardly see the layout. It looked like a *dog's breakfast.* When the wheelchair with the dead guy went by us, the player immediately to my left started yelling at me. He said I had shortchanged him. He had covered the numbers with five- and ten-dollar bets, and he said I had shorted him on a column bet. He reached over and, with his index fingernail, pushed over his five-dollar chip stack and on the bottom was one of our maroon five-hundred-dollar chips. He was yelling that I owed him a thousand dollars."

"And did we?"

"No, sir. No way."

"How do you know he didn't have the five-hundred-dollar chip on the bottom of his stack?"

"I just know."

"How?"

"Well, with respect Chance. I've seen this movie before. I've been in this business six years, and I know how players try to past-post roulette dealers. The most problematic are those players who are closest to the dealers. They know that once the pea is lodged on the number in the slot, and the dealer leans over to pay the bets up by the wheel, the layout and the bets on it are hidden for an instant. That's when they try their scam. In a flash, they'll increase their bet by slipping a high-denomination chip under one of their chips that are already on the layout. These crooks are marvels at how fast they can maneuver their chips while the dealer is bent over, reaching across the layout to collect the losing chips."

"So how do you know he was trying to scam you this time?"

"Because I look. I use the Walter Gretzky method." Declan laughed.

"What the hell is that?"

"Anybody here from Canada?" Declan asked.

"Almost all of us."

"Well, then, you know Wayne's father. Walter was very instrumental in Wayne's development. Growing up I knew pretty early that I was never going to be a great hockey player like him, but I still hung on any word that Wayne, or his Dad said.

"I must have been about ten, and I was watching Hockey Night in Canada when they interviewed Walter. He said one of the tips he gave his son was that Wayne should know where all the players were on the ice, at all times. He said that Wayne should be able to shut his eyes at any time, and *still* know where all the players were. And somehow it just stuck with me. When I became a casino dealer, I taught myself to memorize all the bets on the layout before every spin. I'm pretty good at it, so I can usually tell you the amount of each bet on my layout before the dealer spins the wheel and drops the pea."

"But you're saying usually. *Usually* isn't *always*. How did you know for sure that this guy slipped a five-hundred-dollar maroon chip under his stack of reds after the pea stopped in the slot when you weren't looking? You could have glanced up when the wheelchair went by."

"I did glance up for a second, but it didn't matter because I *always* look down and along the layout to memorize the bets closest to me. I know that's where we are most vulnerable to being cheated, so I memorize the amount of each bet. And I can *tell* you he didn't have no five-hundred-dollar chip under that pile."

"What did you do then?"

"I called for the pit boss, and security was there almost instantly. They quietly hustled him away."

"Comments, guys?" I asked. "Nothing? Well, I'm impressed. Thanks for the summary, Declan. But now I want to hear what happened to the rip-off artist."

"Chance, before I leave, may I ask a question?" interjected Declan.

"Sure, go ahead."

"Why on earth do we have five-hundred-dollar chips? And if we have to have them, why aren't they bright florescent green or orange? The maroon color that they are now is too close to the color of our five-dollar chip. With respect, I think we're taking an unnecessary risk.

"Good comment, Declan. We'll take your suggestion into consideration, and I'll let you know what we decide. And thanks again," I said sincerely. "All right, Norm, bring me up to date about what happened back in the Garden."

The Garden is a twenty-by-twenty room built onto the electrical and maintenance building behind the casino and in the far corner of the parking lot. It's decorated beautifully, if you like sparse. It has precisely one desk, two chairs, a plastic couch, and two five-foot-long terrariums. One is filled with seven harmless snakes and the other with three black widow spiders and six scorpions.

This room exists for only one reason: it is where we bring suspected cheaters. When male guests are brought into the Garden, they are stripped down to their underwear. Women are extended a few more courtesies and are allowed to remain fully clothed, san shoes. But anyone taken to the Garden, male or female, is invited to sit on the couch and told that they will be questioned in *"just a little while."* They are then left there for about two hours with nothing to do except contemplate their indiscretion and maybe read an old newspaper that has been left on the couch. Its headline story is grisly. It's about the gruesome discovery of a body on the east end of the island. It had been eaten by dogs.

By the time Norm returns to conduct the interview, the perp is usually all too happy to provide the details of their cheating. In the few cases where the people won't provide the entire details, they are asked whether they prefer snakes or spiders. Once they provide their answer, Norm removes the end glass panel from that particular terrarium and starts to leave the room. He never gets very far. When those creatures began to leave the glass enclosure, it's amazing how quickly the perps cooperate. Once Norm has the information and a signed confession, they are photographed. The photo is then provided to the Disguise Detection System organization in Las Vegas and circulated to its seven thousand members around the world.

At this point, the bad guys are free to get dressed and leave, but *wonder of wonders,* before they go, they seem to always want to *donate* money and casino chips to the Mary Star of the Sea Church. They also invariably ask when it would be OK for them to leave the island. We usually give them back a hundred dollars and say, "Anytime you like…and don't let the door hit you in the ass on the way out." You can bet they are out of the Garden and off the island like they have been shot from a cannon, and hopefully we will never see any of them in our Diamond Resorts casinos again.

"Chance, as usual, we didn't have any issues with the guy who was trying to take us down. His name is Kurt Peters. He's a well-known cheater around the world. DDS has sent us many pictures of him in the disguises that he uses, including some of him in drag," said Norm. "He's a pro. Once we walked into the Garden, he knew things weren't going to be pretty so he fessed up right away. No issues. He dropped all his cash and chips into the donation box and after taking pictures we were out of there. The entire process didn't take 10 minutes."

When Norm mentioned that the six-foot-two, two-twenty-pound cheater had dressed up in women's clothes, everyone laughed at the mental image. But George chimed in, "Former world champion boxer, Oscar Bonaventure, used to dress up in drag as did former head of the FBI, J. Edgar Hoover. So I guess if they can do it, anyone can!"

After the laughter had subsided I said, "This is really our first major cheating episode, and it illustrates just how far people will go to steal from casinos. Let's make sure we don't let it happen again."

Chapter Twenty-Three

Life is what happens when you're busy making other plans.
—Anonymous

Debbie was now really showing visible signs of her pregnancy. We were both thrilled and looking forward to presenting Rylee with a little brother or sister. With typical overprotectiveness, I tried to get her to slow down a little, but she kept going like a whirlwind.

One evening at dinner she said, "Chance, what would you think about me going over to Miami for the day, sometime next week?"

I was a little surprised and asked, "What for?"

"Christmas isn't too far off," she said. "I want to go over while there is still a good selection of toys available. We need a lot for the local kids for our parish Christmas party. We have the funds from the charity event to spend, but there's not much variety in the shops here. I'd love to do up the party really well and give the kids a really happy day."

Typical Debbie. Generous and giving. No wonder I was so crazy about her.

"I think that's great, Deb," I said, squeezing her hand. "But you can't do it all by yourself. Why don't I clear my schedule for a couple of days and come with you? We can make it a little getaway just for the two of us."

"I'm not going by myself," she said. And then she took a dramatic pause, as if she were a magician going for the *reveal*. "Maria's going with me."

I couldn't believe it.

"How the hell did she convince Raymundo to let her go?"

Debbie said, "When Raymundo's taking drugs, he's a monster to her. But when he's sober, sometimes he feels ashamed of the way he treats her. I think she caught him at just the right time and he said OK."

I just hoped he wouldn't change his mind before they left. I said, "What about their little girl? Is she coming too?"

"No," Debbie said, her eyes darkening. "Raymundo still knows that Maria would escape if she could. So he will keep their daughter here..."

"...like a hostage?" I ventured.

Debbie nodded. "Just like a hostage."

I tried to lighten the mood a little. I smiled and said, "Well, at least you will have some fun on the mainland. But not too much fun I hope. I don't want to hear about you two closing down the bars and flirting with all the college boys."

Debbie laughed. "Oh yeah, nothing a college boy likes more than a fat pregnant lady who's old enough to be their...um... older sister."

"No," I said, "but they love beautiful women. And you're the most beautiful woman I've ever seen."

Debbie leaned across the table and gave me a sweet kiss.

"You're a liar," she said, "but I love you for it."

We talked a little about the logistics of the trip—when they'd be leaving and returning and where they'd be staying. I told her that I would get their plane tickets so she wouldn't have to worry about it.

The day before they were to leave, Debbie again mentioned the flight details and was musing about her time of arrival in Miami. I could see she was fighting her fear of flying. I could also see that she was doing everything she could to keep her growing panic from showing.

"I have a surprise for you," I said. "I've arranged for you and Maria to fly over in King's Own Resort's private plane."

"Oh, you didn't have to do that," she said.

I shrugged. "It's a nice gesture by King's Own Resort. You did some very valuable work for the casino when we were putting together the charity event, and we're grateful. Using the company plane is a bit of a thank you, and it will save you some expense."

Debbie smiled and said, "You mean it'll save *you* some expense."

"You caught me." I laughed. "Anyway, it means more toys for the kids, right?"

"Thanks, Chance. I'll tell Maria."

The next morning I spent a little time driving Debbie crazy, making sure she had packed everything, checking to see that she had her passport, and asking last-minute questions about things she needed me to do while she was gone.

"Oh, I look forward to the peace and quiet of the airplane," she said, and I was pleased to see that she made the little joke without looking scared to death about the flight.

"So sue me," I said. "I'm going to miss you. I want to make sure everything is all right."

Debbie smiled and put her arms around my neck. "I'll be home in less than forty-eight hours. You won't even have time to notice I've gone."

"You're probably right," I said. "I'll be living my hot bachelor lifestyle and the time will fly."

"Well, remember that your hot bachelor lifestyle includes taking Rylee to the dentist tomorrow."

We kissed and I took her bags out to the car.

The gals were departing from the small terminal used by private aircraft located on the far side of the airport away from the main terminal. All noncommercial aircraft were parked, stored and serviced here. It was incredibly convenient to be able to pull right up to the door to off-load baggage and passengers. Still it wasn't like the old days when you could walk someone right to the gate, but it was nice nevertheless to be able to say good-byes without the hassles of the main terminal. The entire unhurried scene probably contributed to Debbie's reduced stress level. In fact, I wouldn't even have known she was anxious except that she only stopped chatting long enough to take a breath. Man, she could sure talk when she was nervous. She reminded me three times that this was just a short hop over to Florida. No big deal.

When I pulled up to the airport curb, I saw that Raymundo's long black Lincoln was already there. He and Maria were talking at the curb, and if you didn't know better, you'd have thought they were a loving couple saying a fond farewell to each other.

Debbie said, "I hoped he wouldn't be here."

"Just be nice and polite," I said. "We don't want him changing his mind at the last minute."

Raymundo greeted us warmly even though this was the first time I had seen him since the episode at the poker table with Greg. *No lingering sense of embarrassment with this guy,* I thought.

Maria and Debbie embraced. Debbie turned to me and said, "I'll call you later." Then she gave me a kiss, and she and Maria walked into the small terminal, chatting nervously but happy.

Raymundo smiled and waved as they walked away. As soon as they were through the automatic glass doors, his smile disappeared.

"I hope you warned your wife that she'd better not try anything funny on this trip," he said.

I looked him right in the eye, but I was nervous bordering on terrified. This man had armed goons who could make me disappear with only a nod.

"They're just doing some Christmas shopping, Raymundo," I said. "They're not trying anything."

"Your bitch of a wife has already tried to get Maria away from me once," Raymundo said.

I stepped forward. Fear or not, I was going to flatten him.

The doors of the limo opened, and without a word, two of his bodyguards stepped out and stood on either side of me.

Raymundo smiled a sinister smile. "If she tries again, it's going to be the last thing she does."

I said hoarsely, "Listen, Padrino, if you even come near my wife, I'll kill you."

"Watch the threats, little man," he said. "You might just scare me to death." He made a motion, and the two bodyguards stepped aside as he got into the limo, laughing. They followed him in. The car drove away, while I stood there trembling in anger.

Chapter Twenty-Four

There can be no greater pain than to outlive your children.
—Author Colette Kelly

There was plenty of work to be done at the office, although I wasn't in the mood to do it. We had just received the operations casino reports from the other eight casinos, and I was anxious to see the month-over-month comparisons against the previous year. And I still had to closely monitor Johnny's activities. But I also knew I needed to get my mind off the confrontation with Raymundo. So I went in and tried to immerse myself in the thousand details that needed my attention.

Barry and I had decided we could best keep an eye on Johnny by keeping him busy here in San Vida, so we asked him to ramp up our dealer's school so we could put more trainees through. However, nobody had seen him that morning. I tried calling him a couple of times, but it went to voicemail. *Maybe he's hungover*, I thought. Or maybe he was just pulling another one of those passive-aggressive moves that had been cropping up more and more often recently. I had avoided any confrontation so far, but I was going to have to talk with him soon. I would keep it friendly and somewhat innocuous, but I had to confront him on some level, or my lack of attention would set off *his* alarm bells. It was a dance similar to that of the cobra and the mongoose. We both knew that something was going on. But only time would tell how it was going to play out.

The workday seemed to stretch out forever and by four o'clock I'd had enough. I wanted to get home and kick back. It occurred to me that Debbie and Maria should have landed in Miami a few hours ago. Debbie had promised to call, but I still hadn't heard anything. *Oh well*, I thought, *she is probably giddy with the idea of rushing all over Miami, spending my money, and just forgot.*

I was feeling leisurely, so the usual six-minute drive to my house took seven. I parked in the driveway and entered the house through the side door into the kitchen.

The house was filled with the kind of silence you notice immediately, even if you can't quite put your finger on why. I called out, "Marilyn, Rylee? Anybody home?"

They must have gone to the market to get some last-minute item for dinner, I thought. But in an instant I knew it was more than that. There was a broken bowl on the floor and one of the kitchen chairs was lying on its side. From there to the back door where I was standing, there were drops of blood. My mind raced for an explanation. Rylee must have dropped the bowl and cut herself and Marilyn had driven her to the emergency room. Or maybe Marilyn had cut herself.

That's when I saw the note on the kitchen table.

"No cops or they both die."

It was handwritten on an index card. I stared at it, but it made no sense. I couldn't get my head around what was happening.

Then my brain snapped into focus. I pulled out my phone and jabbed at the keypad.

"Norm!" I yelled, the panic rising in my voice. "Marilyn and Rylee have been kidnapped. That son of a bitch has taken my little girl!"

"What son of a bitch?"

"It's gotta be Raymundo!"

Chapter Twenty-Five

Denial ain't just a river in Egypt.
—Mark Twain

Norm, Johnny, Sy and I sat in my living room, staring at one another helplessly. We knew we had to make a plan. But what?

Norm wondered aloud, "Are you sure we shouldn't just call the police? Greg can keep this under his hat."

I shook my head. "The note said no cops. Raymundo has enough eyes on his payroll to watch us every step of the way."

"Yeah," said Johnny. "We don't want them to start delivering fingers and shit like that."

Sy growled, "Are you crazy? Just shut up!"

"What?" exclaimed Johnny.

"That's a little girl you're talking about. Just shut up about fingers."

Johnny held up both hands in the classic "I surrender" gesture and then leaned back on the couch.

"So what do we do?" I asked. "Is there a way to follow Raymundo or something like that? Can we get a GPS on his car?"

Norm shook his head. "It'll be tough to get a GPS on his car, but anyway, wherever they're being held, he ain't going there. He'll have some of his goons standing guard."

Johnny said, "Even if we figure out where they are, how are we going to outgun these mothers?"

The doorbell rang, Norm answered the door, and Ozzie strolled in.

Oblivious to the circumstances, he greeted everyone in his familiar manner. "Hey guys, what's up? What's goin' on?"

Everybody was puzzled by his arrival. Everybody except Sy.

With no explanation, Sy simply said, "Ozzie, we gotta take a drive."

Sy turned to me. "I've got an idea. Keep your phone on. When I call you, you gotta be ready to jump."

"What are you doing, Sy?" I asked.

Sy just held up his hand and walked out the door, followed by a quizzical Ozzie.

Once they were in the car, Ozzie asked, "Where to?"

"We're going to Twelve Mile Rock," Sy said.

Ozzie shook his head. "You're kidding. You want to go into the native settlements? What's up?" he asked.

Sy filled Ozzie in on the kidnapping. Ozzie's eyes flashed with fury.

"Turn around, Sy," said Ozzie.

"What do you mean turn around?"

Ozzie said, "Just turn around. I'll go, but you ain't going wid me. You look like a baseball in a load of coal. Nobody say nothin' if you dere. I go alone."

"Are you thinking what I'm thinking?" Sy asked.

Ozzie nodded. "Gotta be Waiterman."

Ever since Sy had been robbed on the golf course, Sy and Ozzie had been conducting their own investigation. It had taken some time, but they thought they were close to nailing the perps. They'd only recently figured out that the guy behind the heist was a Balboan named Waiterman. Several years earlier, he had worked at the golf-club bar, so he knew about the golf wagers, the poker and card games, and who carried heavy coin. Waiterman had recruited talent from Playas to pull the job, and as soon as it was done, they had split the proceeds, and his cohorts disappeared like a puff of smoke.

Ozzie and Sy had learned that this wasn't his first robbery. He had also supplied the guns and hired the guys to rob the Emeralds of Colombia jewelry store in the bazaar about six months earlier. Afterward, the robbers had stayed at his place for a few days to let things cool down before they scooted off the island. Knowing all this made Waiterman the odds-on favorite to have been behind this kidnapping.

"Sy, I've done time and everybody know me. I'll find out."

"OK. But when you've got a handle on anything, let me know right away."

"You bet, mon. You'll get your shot."

"I figure this might take you a few hours," Sy said. "That'll give me time to make another stop."

"Where?" Ozzie asked.

"Waiterman isn't the only suspect," Sy said. "Chance is sure that Raymundo did it."

"And you goin' up against Raymundo—just you and him?"

Sy curled his lip and said, "Yeah, it doesn't seem fair to Raymundo, does it?"

Sy dropped Ozzie back at his own car, and they drove away in opposite directions.

Back at the house, Norm, Johnny, and I kept batting around ideas. Eventually Norm said, "Chance, we all want to do everything we can to help, and I hate to bring this up, but someone needs to look in on the casino. There's a storm front coming through, and there's no telling how bad it could be. We could lose our power, even our backup generator. And we need to ensure the cash and chips are in the safe and the count room is secured."

Johnny spoke up. "Yeah, Norm, you're right. I can stay here with Chance. Why don't you go and keep your ears open there as well? We'll keep you informed."

"Damn, I totally forgot about the casino," I said. "You guys are right. If this storm knocks out the power there, we could have all kinds of security problems. Somebody should go. But I think it should be you, Johnny. You're the one best able to deal with our back-up auxiliary generators and all that stuff."

"Well, OK, Chance. I'd rather stay here, though."

"No, go. If there's anything major, contact Norm. And thanks. Thanks for your concern and your help."

Expressing his reluctance, Johnny finally left for the casino. Maybe I had misjudged him. He had been helpful and supportive, and we needed everyone involved. I was so consumed with the kidnapping that it took a while before it dawned on me that I still hadn't heard from Debbie. She had to have been in Miami for close to ten hours and still not a word. That wasn't like her at all.

I had a dull ache in the pit of my stomach. I had Norm call a local air traffic controller we knew to make sure their plane had arrived in Miami OK, which it had. In the meantime, I called their hotel.

"Yes," said the pleasant voice on the line, "we have that reservation, but Mrs. Daly hasn't checked in."

"Are you sure?" I asked, immediately realizing what a stupid question it was.

"Yes, sir. Can I do anything else for you?"

"Yes, I'm Chance Daly, Mrs. Daly's husband. Please leave a note for my wife to call me the second she gets in."

As I hung up, I had a cold feeling of dread. Marilyn and Rylee kidnapped and Debbie missing? It couldn't be a coincidence.

My phone rang, and before I could say hello, Sy started in, "Come down to the docks. I'll meet you at warehouse number seven."

"What's going on, Sy?"

He said, "Just get here, and get here now."

I disconnected and turned to Norm.

"That was Sy. Something's up. Stay here. I'll call you as soon as I know what going on."

I drove as fast as I could toward the harbor. Many of the warehouses in that area were dilapidated and abandoned. At the far end I found number seven, and in front of its large metal doors sat Sy's car.

I parked beside it and approached the building cautiously. When I eased open one of the doors, I was greeted with almost complete darkness. I stepped in, nervous, but saw a very dim light at the far end of the cavernous building, and the silhouette of someone standing.

"Chance!" It was Sy's voice. "Watch your step. There's junk all over the floor."

I picked my way toward Sy's voice and soon was close enough to see that the dim light was coming from a large flashlight set on the floor. Caught in its white beam was Sy. And in front of Sy, tied to a chair, was Raymundo. There was something jammed in his mouth, which was mostly covered with duct tape, and his pants were draped around his ankles.

"Sy!" I exclaimed. "What's this? What's going on?"

Sy motioned me away. Raymundo made loud grunts from his chair, as if he were trying to yell threats at us.

Once we were several yards away, Sy spoke to me in a hoarse whisper. "You like Raymundo for this kidnapping, right?"

"Well, yeah, but—"

"But nothing," Sy interrupted. "He needs to tell us where Marilyn and Rylee are and he needs to tell us *now*. I've been working on him a bit, so he knows I'm serious."

"Are you beating it out of him?"

Sy glanced back over at the writhing man. "You got a better idea?"

"How did you even get him here?" I asked. "Where are his bodyguards?"

"Lucky me," Sy said. "There was only one bodyguard. Raymundo was being driven probably over to the golf course or to the casino. They turned down a backstreet, and *we had a slight fender bender*. When the driver got out of the car, I popped him. Then I dragged Raymundo out of his car, banged him around a little, zip-tied his hands, and put him in my backseat."

"How did you—?"

"Yeah, yeah, I know what you're thinking," Sy cut me off. "I ain't stronger than Raymundo. Not normally, anyway. Lucky for me he was pretty drugged up. It wasn't that hard."

"Did anybody see you?" I wondered aloud.

"Yeah, a couple of druggies. I tossed them Raymundo's wallet. Told them they could have whatever they found on the bodyguard—and they could camp in his Caddy for all I cared."

"Holy shit!" I burst out, and I had never meant it more.

We stood there in silence for a long moment.

"So has he told you anything?"

"Nope. He's making a pretty convincing argument that he doesn't know nothing about nothing. I even tried something that's usually totally persuasive."

Sy walked over to Raymundo and picked something up off the floor. Raymundo flinched violently when he saw it. No doubt his muffled sounds were screams. Sy turned and handed me the object.

"This looks like…good God…is this an orange squeezer?"

Sy cackled. "A little low-tech, I know. But effective. Never known it to fail. You stick their balls in there, squeeze the handles, and what comes out ain't orange juice."

I didn't even want to imagine the kind of agony that thing would cause.

"But here's the thing, Chance. Even with that, he insists he doesn't know dick about any of this. Man, he was whining like a baby. He was begging me to stop. But he didn't admit a thing. I hate to say this, but…" Sy looked at Raymundo, who glared back at him with red eyes. "…I'm beginning to think he didn't have anything to do with it."

Sy's phone rang. He glanced down at it and said, "It's Ozzie." Then into the phone, he asked, "What's going on?"

"Waiterman know sometin. He one whacked-out motha fuckin' dude, but he know sometin fo' sure."

"Where is he?"

"I got eyes on him," Ozzie said. "He been doin' coke for tree straight days. I know da bar where he at. We can snatch him, OK?"

"I know where we need to take him," Sy said.

"Where?"

"The Stoned Crab. They're closed on Mondays. It's the perfect place."

Sy disconnected and said to me, "I gotta go. Don't let this asshole outta your sight."

"What was that about the Stoned Crab?"

Sy was already heading for the door. "I'll let you know when there's something for you to know. Stay here with Raymundo." Sy reached into his waistband, pulled out a .38, and handed it to me. This is only for emergencies. As much as you might want to put one in his ear, don't do anything stupid. We may still need him."

"I don't need it. I got this one from the console in my car," I said, showing him the gun that Norm had stashed there.

As fast as the rapidly deteriorating conditions would allow, Sy headed to the bar where Ozzie had spotted Waiterman. The wind had come up, and it was blowing so hard that it was difficult to keep the car heading straight, especially at high speeds. As soon as Sy saw Ozzie's car, he pulled alongside, and Ozzie jumped in.

"Did you hear da latest?" Ozzie asked.

"What's that?"

"Dere's a small, fast-movin' tropical storm coming tru. It's tracking due nort. No tellin' whether it cut west to Florida or head to us, but it's de last ting we need."

Sy glanced down at the bag that Ozzie was holding in his lap. "Whatcha got?"

"Coke," Ozzie said. "We goin' fishin' for info. We need bait."

"Man, it sure is getting ugly," said Sy. "With this wind kicking up, you know the rain isn't far behind."

Ozzie said, "You oughta call Norm. May need him. Tell him to meet us."

Sy nodded and punched in the number. When Norm answered, Sy said, "Meet us at the Stoned Crab in…"

"There's Waiterman," Ozzie said, pointing ahead. The man was just coming out of the bar, weaving in the wind like a scarecrow. Half of his unsteadiness was cocaine, the other half the wind.

Sy continued into the phone, "...ten minutes. No time for questions."

Sy pulled his car up to Waiterman, who seemed unsure about which car he should get into.

"Hey buddy," Ozzie said jovially, "we gon party. Come on wit us!"

Waiterman looked closely at Ozzie's face as if he had never seen him before. Sy began to think how they could overpower him and get him into the car, but then Waiterman grinned.

"Ozzie, right?" Waiterman said. "Ozzie buddy..."

"Yeah, mon," Ozzie said. "I got a big bag o' coke, and we're headed to da party where they's pussy every which way you look. Want in?"

Waiterman was too stoned to know what he wanted. Ozzie eased the back door open. Finally, Waiterman almost fell in.

"Gimme a line," Waiterman said.

Ozzie glanced at him over his shoulder. "Patience, my friend. We can't do no line in da jumpy car. You don' wanna spill all dis sweet powder, do you?"

"I wanna bump!" Waiterman insisted.

"You getta bump soon. Wid all da party pussy, you goin be banging like a screen door inna hurricane. We almost dere," Ozzie said. "All be dere soon."

Waiterman started pounding Ozzie's back. "I want it now, motha! Now!"

Sy pulled over abruptly. He got out of the car, opened the rear door, and grabbed Waiterman by the hair. He pushed his face into the back of the front seat and, with the butt of his automatic, whacked him hard on the side of his head.

But real life isn't like the movies where a single knock on the head makes someone instantly unconscious. In this instance, Waiterman just collapsed in pain, disoriented, and started moaning.

"Sy, you sho can be a problem solver," said Ozzie. "Remind me not to cross you."

Minutes later, they pulled into the parking lot of the Stoned Crab. It was deserted except for Norm's car.

As Norm approached them, Sy gestured toward the back seat. "A little help here, Norm."

The three of them dragged the dazed Waiterman onto the deserted restaurant patio deck overlooking the crashing waves.

"OK, you wacko, tell us where the kid and the grandma are!" Norm yelled over the noise of the surf. "This is your big chance. Don't blow it!" He pushed Waiterman's arm up behind him.

But Waiterman only screamed, "Ain't telling you nothin'! Get me outta here and den I tell you!"

"Ain't gonna happen. Tell us now, and we'll let you go. If you don't talk, you're shark bait." Ozzie and Norm each grabbed a leg and held a writhing Waiterman over the water.

How or why the sharks began to gather is anyone's guess, but in seconds, three or four could be seen in the frothing ocean only ten feet below Waiterman's terrified head.

"Don' drop me! Take me up!" he screamed.

As Ozzie and Norm began to slowly bring him back up, Ozzie said, "Where dey be, where are dey?"

"At de church. At de old church up Government Road by de ridge."

"I know de one," said Ozzie. "It be boarded up for years." He leaned down toward Waiterman's face. "De one by de old orchard?"

212

"Yah! Dat be de one. Now lemme go!"

"And who's in this with you?" said Sy as he pushed Ozzie away and grabbed Waiterman's leg. "Who else?"

"I'll tell you, but you gotta bring me up first."

"Gimme a name or you're goin down! Gimme a name!" yelled Sy as he pumped Waiterman's legs as if he were going to drop him.

"Johnny! Johnny A!" Waiterman cried, his voice a strangled plea.

Sy, Norm, and Ozzie looked at one another. "Johnny A. Why would he do that?" demanded Sy.

Waiterman nearly sobbed. "De whole ting be his idea. He tol' me Chance broke his tumbs for no good reason. Said he was going to make 'im pay." He writhed crazily and begged, "Now pull me up."

"Norm, give him to me. Let me take him," Sy said. Norm released his grip a little, and Sy took him. Once he had both legs, Sy shook him a little as if to get a better grip and then let go. "Oops!" was all he said.

The screams didn't last long and could barely be heard over the wind, the waves, and the storm.

With the wind now howling, the three men turned as one and began to run back to their cars. The building had given them protection from the buffeting wind, but as soon as they rounded the corner, the gale force pushed them back so hard they could barely make any headway. While on the patio deck, they had been on the lee side of the building and hadn't noticed how the wind had morphed into a full-fledged tropical storm. Hunched over and whipped by the sheets of rain, they struggled getting to their cars and, once there, could barely pry their doors open.

"I'll follow you!" yelled Norm, and with great effort, they climbed in.

It was hard keeping their cars on the road as they made their way up Sunshine Highway to San Vida. Driving as fast as conditions allowed, they picked their way through broken tree branches, a couple of trailers, chain-link fence sections and other wreckage from the storm that was now littering the roads.

Sy said, "Ozzie, get Chance on the phone. I'd better let him know what's going on. At least about the girls. I'm not going to tell him about Johnny yet. It can't help now, and it might hurt big-time if he goes crazy on us."

Chapter Twenty-Six

Sometimes you just have to do what you have to do.
Chuck Connolly, Dallas Texas

In the meantime, I had found another chair in the corner of the warehouse and carried it over, setting it down about two yards in front of Raymundo.

"I'm going to take the gag off. If you try anything stupid, I'll shoot you in the head. Do you understand me, Padrino?"

Raymundo's eyes burned through me, but he nodded.

I ripped off the duct tape, enjoying the wince of pain on his face as it tore on his whiskers.

"You're in a world of shit," he said.

I said, "You're the one tied to a chair, and I'm the one pointing a gun at your ugly head. Now tell me what you've done with my family."

Raymundo glared at me. "I'll tell you what I told that senile old motherfucker. I don't know what you're talking about." His eyes took on another look. Fear? Or maybe it was just fatigue. "I've done nothing."

"You threaten me regarding my wife and then she disappears?" I jammed the gun barrel into his temple. "My daughter and my mother-in-law get kidnapped? You're the one who said you would hurt my wife. You!"

Raymundo shook his head. "Your wife was messing with my marriage. She didn't have any business trying to talk my wife into leaving me. I just wanted her to leave us alone. But I wouldn't kill her. Why would I do that? What kind of sense does that make? And what's that about a kidnapping? When did that happen? I don't know anything about any kidnapping."

My cell phone rang. I held it to my ear and stepped away from Raymundo.

"What's up?"

Ozzie handed the phone to Sy. "We know where they are," Sy said.

I was almost too stunned, and too relieved, to reply.

"Where?"

"At an old, abandoned church up Government Road. Come as fast as you can. We may need your gun."

"What do I do with Raymundo?" I asked.

"It looks like he didn't have anything to do with the kidnapping," Sy said. "But we still don't know what he might have done with Debbie. Leave him there. We'll go back and sort things out after we get Marilyn and Rylee."

I strode back over to Raymundo and picked up the gag and duct tape.

"What are you—?"

I crammed the cloth into his mouth and wrapped the tape over it.

"Sit tight," I said. "I'll be back." I leaned in close to him. "And when I get back, if you don't tell me where my wife is, this warehouse will be the last place you will ever see."

I had been so wrapped up in my confrontation with Raymundo that I'd barely noticed the howling wind growing in ferocity. I could barely get the metal door to open against the force, but I finally squeezed through the narrow opening and ran to the car. I knew roughly where the abandoned church was—Ozzie had pointed the road out to me one day when we were touring the island. But tonight the air was so filled with limbs, leaves, and sheets of rain that I knew I would have trouble finding anything.

When they turned off onto the church road, Sy pulled over to let Norm catch up. When he did, Sy yelled to him to park his car and climb in. Once in the car, Sy told Norm that Chance was on his way and that he hadn't told him about Johnny, only the whereabouts of the girls.

"I don't know, Sy. I think we need to tell him. I would've done it already, but my phone's dead," said Norm.

And as the magnitude of what had happened with Waiterman hit him, Norm turned to Sy in shock and anguish and said, "And *what happened* back there? I'm just *saying!* I'm just saying. Did we have to do that? Why'd we do that?"

When Norm had exhausted his tirade, Sy looked across the front seat and said, "Who cares about that piece of shit? He *kidnapped* Rylee and Marilyn! So screw him! He's gone. The world's a better place. Anyway, nobody saw nothing. Nobody saw us pick him up. Nobody. But if anybody asks or gets on us for any reason, as far as I'm concerned, we had him at the Stoned Crab, slapped him around a bit, got the info we needed and he slipped away from us. In the storm and confusion, we lost him. If he didn't make it out of the parking lot, then maybe he got swept out to sea, and that's too bad for him. Isn't that what happened to Waiterman?" asked Sy, glancing back to Ozzie in the backseat.

"Waiterman who?" was all Ozzie said.

"Yeah. Ozzie's got it right. That's the best way to handle it. *Waiterman who?* Anyway, what's done is done. Let's find the girls. And we can tell Chance about Johnny as soon as we get them back," Sy said with considerable authority. "He's on his way and he'll have a gun with him. We need all the firepower we can get. But now that we *think* we know where they are, I'm wondering if we should have waited and brought Greg in on this. We don't know what we're up against here."

"But then we would have had to tell him about Waiterman, and our lives might become a hell of a lot more complicated," said a very subdued Norm.

Bumping along the road, and presumably getting closer to the church, Ozzie became increasingly agitated.

"What's with you, Ozzie?" asked Sy. "First Norm and now you?"

"Dogs, man," Ozzie said. "I hate dem dogs. Dat church be up by de old dump. Sometimes dat where de dogs hang. Dogs bad. Dey eat us fo' sure."

Sy grunted and shook his head. He had never experienced fear himself, so he didn't really understand it in others.

"Ozzie," Norm said, "the one good thing about this storm is that the dogs won't be roaming. They don't like the rain any more than we do. They'll be holed up in a cave somewhere."

"Yeah, maybe you right, white bread. Dey probably won't eat black meat before white meat anyway, so let's go." He looked over at Norm and Sy. "But just in case, you go first…"

Sy said, "I have a shovel in the trunk, so one of you grab that when we stop. Norm, take a look in the glove box. There's a flashlight in there."

Norm opened the compartment. "Got it."

The way to the church used to be a single-lane dirt road, but as the rain pounded harder, the dirt turned to nothing but giant puddles and mud. Sy's car wasn't an all-terrain vehicle, not by a long shot, and every second he expected that they'd get mired and stuck in place.

Then, just ahead, a large dark shape loomed in a clearing.

"Dere it is!" exclaimed Ozzie. "Da church."

The three men sat there for a minute, trying to scope out the scene. It was too dark to see much, and there was no light coming from the windows. The building was as black as a grave and only illuminated by the occasional flash of lightning.

But then, from behind them, silhouetted by one flash, they saw an approaching vehicle. Sy took their only pistol from his shoulder holster and all three bailed out of the car, and eased behind the tree line.

Suddenly Norm breathed a big sigh of relief. "It's Chance," he said.

I saw Sy's car just ahead and pulled over to the side of the road and drove up on some fallen palm fronds and branches, hoping they would make a firmer place to park. I had shut off the car's interior light, so it remained dark as I opened the door. I joined the guys, and all four of us moved behind one of the mounds of garbage that had accumulated over the years. We were hidden from the church—at least as far as we could tell.

"Any signs of life?" I asked.

"No, but do you have your gun?" Sy asked.

"Yeah, I've got it. So what's our move?" We were being pelted with rain, and all four of us looked as if we'd just had a long swim, fully dressed.

"I think the best thing to do is to surround the church and move in from four sides," Norm whispered.

"We're going to surround the church with four guys, two guns and a shovel? Lets hope there aren't too many of them."

"It's what we've got," Sy said. "We only have two guns between us, so for Christ's sake, don't shoot anything until you're sure what, or who, you've got in your sights."

Suddenly, silence enveloped us. We were in the eye of the tropical depression. In the center of even the worst depression or hurricane, there is an eerie calm. This was it. The wind and the rain stopped, replaced by dead quiet air. The eye of the storm gave us a break, and we heard a *bang, thump, bang, thump* from inside. There was only a faint glow of light from the rising sun, but it was enough. I eased the church door open, the .38 in my hand. Nothing happened. No one shot me, or attacked me, and just a few yards in front of me, I could just barely make out Rylee and Marilyn bound and gagged on the floor. Marilyn had been kicking an old metal file cabinet, making the only noise she could.

I yelled "THEY'RE HERE!" as the guys rushed in.

We quickly untied them. Rylee was wailing loudly from fear, discomfort, and confusion. Marilyn and I were crying too but from relief.

After relieved cries of greetings all around, all I could say was, "Let's get our girls home."

I asked Norm to drive Rylee, Marilyn, and me home. Ozzie took Norm's keys so they could pick up his car.

Our little procession had barely made it back to the main road, when the winds kicked up again. We maneuvered through the fallen debris back to our place—it was usually a ten-minute drive, but it took us the greater part of thirty. Rylee lay across the back seat with her head in my lap. She was asleep in seconds, and I was grateful. I didn't want her asking for her mommy.

Back at the house, I put Rylee to bed and lay with her awhile, while my comrades waited for me in the living room. Then I prayed. My brain was racked with anguish thinking about what might have happened if we hadn't found them. As I started to get up, I fell to my knees and, with all my heart, thanked God for bringing Rylee home to me. And I sobbed.

It took a few minutes to compose myself and get my brain back in gear. When I got my act together I went back into the living room and handed out some glasses. I gave Norm a bottle of Scotch, which we passed around and each filled their glass and took a drink. We were all just trying to decompress. It was tough to process. I couldn't make any sense of it at all. And I was worried sick about Debbie.

Minutes later, Marilyn came into the living room, and I handed her a glass of Scotch. She downed it in one gulp and then gave me a hard stare.

"All right, Rylee's asleep, tell me. Where's Debbie?"

"I don't know," I confessed. "We're working on it. Maybe Raymundo knows. We've got him in a secure place, and I've got to get back there."

Sy stood up. "No," he said. "You need to stay here with your family. I'll go back and deal with Raymundo."

"OK, Sy," I said. "But like you told me, don't do anything you can't undo. He's the only lead we have."

"Don't worry," Sy said. "He's going to tell me what he knows. Before, I only leaned on him about Rylee and Marilyn. Now I'm gonna go at him real strong about Debbie."

"Norm, Ozzie," I said, "go with him."

"But, Chance, there's other stuff we need to tell you," blurted out Norm.

I only half heard him as Sy interrupted, "We'll bring him up to date as soon as we deal with Raymundo. Let's go."

When they were gone, Marilyn poured herself another shot.

"Chance," she said, "I'm about to start screaming. Where's my daughter?"

I sighed a heavy sigh, "I wish I knew."

As the storm was subsiding, I shared what little I knew. I told her that I suspected that Raymundo was responsible for Debbie's disappearance, and with Sy conducting the interrogation, I was confident that if Raymundo knew anything, anything at all, Sy would get it out of him. I didn't mention *how* Sy would do it, but I did let her know that there was no one better at getting someone to talk.

Understandably, Marilyn had many questions, but I really had nothing more to tell her. After about five minutes, she finally asked what the police thought and what they were doing about it. When I told her that they hadn't been informed, she absolutely freaked. It took several long minutes to calm her down to where she became barely rational again. With her tears and my aching heart, I had no good answers and very few ideas. The best I could do was to tell her that we needed a couple of more hours of leaning on Raymundo, and if we couldn't get a solid lead then we'd get the police involved.

I was exhausted physically and emotionally, when the phone rang.

I had no sooner picked it up when Sy started in on me. "What did you do?" he asked.

"What do you mean?"

"I mean we walk into the warehouse, and Raymundo has a bullet hole right between his eyes. This is really bad, Chance. He coulda told us…"

222

I didn't believe my ears. "He's dead? Are you sure?" I babbled stupidly.

Sy said, "It was right between the eyes, for Christ's sake. So you didn't do this?"

"Of course not," I said. "We needed information from him. I'd never—"

"Well," Sy said, "what's done is done. We'll clean up things here. Starting with getting rid of the body. I guess the good news is that nobody is going to miss him much. If push comes to shove, we can always dump him back at the Stoned Crab."

"What do you mean?" I asked.

"With everything else going on, we haven't had a chance to tell you, but that's where we took Waiterman. He's the one who told us where Rylee and Marilyn were." Sy paused. "And, Chance, he told us something else. He said Raymundo wasn't behind the kidnapping."

"Then who was?"

"You're not going to like this. He said it was Johnny A. And Waiterman wasn't making up stories. I believed him. We wanted to tell you, but at the right time. Norm has been pushing to tell you, but we didn't want you to go nuts on us until we knew more and could work out a plan. At least now you know."

That felt like a dropkick right in the gut. I almost stopped breathing. I knew Johnny was twisted, but I never thought he'd do something like this.

"You're sure?" I asked.

"Absolutely."

"I want to talk to Waiterman."

"You can't."

"What do you mean I can't?" I exploded. "Don't tell me what I can't do. I *want* to!"

"You can't, Chance. Settle down. You can't, as in he's gone. We were working on him. Held him over the water to scare him. And he slipped...he slipped out of my hands. Sorry, buddy, but at least I'm sure he gave us good info."

"Johnny!" I was furious. "Then let's go get the son of a bitch!" I said. "Right now."

Just then I heard our front door push open. What the FU...? With an adrenalin rush and confused with anger and fear, my immediate thought was *my gun*. Where was it? The gun was in the pocket of my wet jacket, draped over a chair in the kitchen. The phone dropped to the floor as I made a desperate dash toward the kitchen. Just as I reached my jacket, but before I could pull out my gun, the door opened. Debbie walked into the living room.

Chapter Twenty-Seven

What evil lurks in the hearts of men?
Only the Shadows know.
—Modified from a radio show of the 1930s

For a stunned second, Marilyn and I just stared at her, unable to move or speak. It was as if we were seeing a ghost. Then Marilyn erupted in a scream, ran across the room, and gripped Debbie in a bear hug, crying and laughing at the same time. When Debbie could pull herself away, I took her in my arms and held her close. I seriously considered never letting her go, *ever*.

While I was kissing my wife all over her face, I heard a faraway voice. I finally realized Sy was shouting into the phone, wondering what in hell was going on. I grabbed it off the floor and yelled into the phone, "Debbie's home! She's fine! You guys get back here!"

It only took Debbie a heartbeat to notice the large bruise on Marilyn's face. "Mom," she asked, "what happened to you?"

Marilyn and I looked at each other and almost started laughing from sheer relief. Marilyn said, "I'm going to have to sit down before I fall down. I think we both have stories to tell."

I don't believe I ever saw a wider range of emotions on anyone's face as Marilyn and I each told our versions of the kidnapping story. Debbie was shocked, then angry, then appalled, and then back to angry. Marilyn could provide no good descriptions of the two villains who burst into the kitchen and took them away. One of them had picked up the child and the other held Marilyn by the shoulders, telling her to come along quietly. Marilyn told us how, when she was being propelled out the kitchen door to a waiting van, she stumbled and, in doing so, pulled herself away from the kidnapper and fell, hitting her head on probably the doorknob. She thought she gave herself the bloody lip then or when she hit the floor.

"So really," Marilyn said, "nobody hit me. I caused the bruise and the blood."

With a grimace I started to say, "Well, the kidnappers had a bit to do with it as well."

But when I got to the part about finding them tied up and lying on the floor at the church, Debbie exploded, "My baby! I've got to see my baby," she said and dashed up the stairs to Rylee's crib. Cradling her sleeping child, now safe and sound in her arms, eventually calmed Debbie down. After five minutes or so, she came back into the living room and sat beside me on the couch. She looked chalk white and drained with exhaustion.

I finished my last bit of the story and her first question was understandable.

"Who did it?" she stammered.

I said, "Listen, Sy's on his way here, and hopefully, he'll have more information. But right now, you need to tell me what happened to you. We've been out of our minds with worry. First Rylee and Marilyn and then you."

Debbie kissed me on the cheek and gave me a concerned smile. "Poor Chance," she said. "All this happening at once. It must have been horrible."

"Where have you been, baby?" I almost sobbed.

Chapter Twenty-Eight

Desperate times sometimes call for desperate measures
—Seymour HarrisRancho Mirage, California

Debbie took a sip of her ice tea, got up from the couch and sat down in a chair facing me and Marilyn.

"I was kidnapped, too," she said, "in a way. But I was never in any danger. Definitely a strange, sometimes terrifying experience, though.

"Everything started out OK. Maria and I had a nice flight over to Miami. She didn't talk about Raymundo at all. It was almost like out of sight, out of mind. It felt to me that she was taking a physical *and* mental break and wasn't going to even think about the terrible turn her life had taken. So I had decided that I would do everything I could to make sure that she had a good time. I think I was so determined to put on my fun face that I almost forgot to be scared of flying. I'd been worrying about it for days before the trip, but I knew that once we got over there and I had a taste of retail therapy, we'd have a blast just hanging out, kind of like a girl's night out. No substance, just shopping and silliness. I knew that it had been a very long time since Maria had been able to do anything like that.

"The flight over was smooth and short. We knew about the storm system coming north, but it was a bit surreal. We were flying in beautiful bright sunshine, but we could look to the south and see the ominous black clouds headed our way. Maria was so upbeat and talkative she was almost giddy, and I thought, 'Wow, she really has forgotten about Raymundo.' Little did I know!

"Even though we were going to be in Miami for only a couple of days, both Maria and I brought extra suitcases to haul back some of the personal things we were going to buy. We were planning to ship the toys via container, but the suitcases were for cosmetics and the girly stuff that's so hard to find here in San Vida. When we landed and deplaned, we headed to the baggage claim area. But while we were walking I noticed this guy watching us. Then I could see that he was staring at us. Then when I made eye contact, he started smiling—definitely smiling *at me, at us.* My first thought was that he had mistaken us for somebody else. But then I noticed Maria smiling back at him. And all of a sudden she ran to him, and they put their arms around each other and started to kiss—like, some *serious necking.* I didn't know what was going on.

"She led him over to me, and they were both beaming from ear to ear. She said, 'This is my friend Debbie.' Then turning to him, she said, 'You know, Chance's wife.' He nodded and shook my hand. 'Pleased to meet you, Debbie. I'm Marco. I know you've been a very good friend to Maria. And we're grateful.' I smiled back at him and said, 'I'm pleased to—wait a minute. Marco? Raymundo's Marco?' Maria replied, 'No, silly, not Raymundo's Marco. *My* Marco!'

"I thought you were...

"'Dead?' he said. 'Yes, a lot of people think that.' He turned to Maria. 'You ready? Which bags are yours?' He motioned to a man standing a few yards away. He came over, and Marco got our baggage-check tickets and gave them to him. 'He'll bring everything to the apartment,' Marco said.

"'But we're staying at a hotel,' I protested.

"'Debbie, Marco's place will be much nicer. You'll have your own room.' I stopped in my tracks. 'What's happening, Maria? What's going on?'

"In a friendly tone, Marco said, 'We'll explain everything to you on the way. But it's very important that we get moving.'

"Initially I refused to budge. Then Maria said, 'Debbie, please. You'll understand everything very soon. This is very important to me.' She looked at me with such hope and looked at Marco with such trust and love that I finally gave up and followed them out to the pickup area. A limo was waiting for us, and the three of us sat in the rear seat.

"As the car began to pull away, I took out my phone. Marco instantly snatched it out of my hand. 'Give that back to me!' I demanded. I was furious. 'I promised Chance I'd call him as soon as we landed.' Marco slipped my phone into his jacket pocket, and as he did, I saw the butt of a pistol in a shoulder holster.

"Marco put his arm around Maria's shoulder and spoke to me in a soft voice. 'I know this seems confusing to you,' he said, 'and I'm sorry it has to go down like this. But it's the only way.'

"'The only way for what?' I demanded.

Maria said, 'Marco and I are in love—we have been for a long time.'

"'Yes, you've told me that,' I replied. 'But I thought Raymundo had him killed.'

"Then Marco said, 'There were several of us who worked for Raymundo who saw that he was getting more and more crazy. Like big-time crazy. I saw the way he treated Maria. I saw the constant bruises and the terror in her eyes. I knew it was only a matter of time until he killed her—maybe accidentally, maybe not. Didn't matter. Either way, she'd be dead.'

"'So Marco started protecting me,' Maria said. 'In little ways, at first. He'd stay close to Raymundo's and my room, and if he heard things getting bad, he'd knock on the door and invent something that Raymundo had to deal with right away. He saved me from beatings more than once. He might even have saved my life. It wasn't long before I fell in love with him. And he with me.'

"Marco kissed the top of her head and said to me, 'In the past I have not lived a good life. I have not been a good man. But Maria made me want to be better. She made me want to change.'

"'We were always very, very careful about seeing each other,' Maria said. 'But eventually Raymundo found out. He gave me a savage beating. I think he broke one of my ribs—it still hurts. And when he was through, he told me that I'd never see Marco again. That he'd had him taken care of. I wanted to die.'

"'But remember I told you that there were several of us who knew that Raymundo would have to be dealt with?' said Marco. 'One of my best friends made Raymundo think that he and I were sworn enemies, and he asked Raymundo for the privilege of being the one to kill me. Raymundo was so blasted on coke that he wasn't even suspicious. He just said to make sure my body was never found. I caught a plane to Miami that night. Didn't pack a bag, just left. My friend reported to Raymundo that he had done the deed. Then a few days later, he told Maria how she could find me.'

"'I was ecstatic,' she said. 'That was the hardest part—not suddenly acting happy. Sometimes Raymundo would beat me just for smiling.'

"Marco said, 'I knew that with your help I could get Maria away from Balboa. But rescuing her little girl would be the hard part.'

230

"'What are you going to do?' I asked. 'I have a plan,' he said. 'I'm waiting for a call to let me know that everything is ready. Then we'll go back to Balboa, get Joanie, and start a new life where nobody knows us.'

"'But Raymundo has Joanie,' I said. 'He'd never let you near her.' "'No, he wouldn't,' Marco agreed. 'But, as I said, I have a plan.'

"A few minutes later, we pulled up to the lavish Ritz Hotel just a block from the beach. We took the elevator up to the twenty-eighth floor penthouse and stepped into an apartment so large that I never actually saw all of it. Maria said there were four bedrooms and five bathrooms. I only saw one of them and the kitchen, and dining room. We sat in a huge living room overlooking Biscayne Bay. It even had a fireplace. As if anybody ever needs to build a fire in Miami.

"'We're going to have to stay up here until I get that call,' Marco said. 'I hope you won't be uncomfortable. Are you hungry? Let's order something from room service.'

"'Can't I please have my phone?' I asked. 'Chance is going to be worried sick.'

"'I'm sorry, I truly am. But if any part of this leaks out before I'm ready to act, the whole thing could blow up. Chance will understand. He'll forgive you and us, once this is all over.'

"We then ordered our food, and I don't know what I expected the room service meal to be, but our lunch was equal to some of the best restaurants I've ever eaten in. Beautifully cooked, served on fine china by two waiters. And remember, I'm eating for two, so don't judge me. I was just about to dive into my food, when Marco's phone rang. He listened for a few seconds and said, 'We'll leave in two hours. Keep your eye on him. Don't let him out of your sight.'

"He turned to us and said, 'We have time for our lunch, but then we will be returning immediately to San Vida. Your luggage will follow later. And Debbie, Maria and I both apologize for making you a part of this. But your involvement was essential, and if we are to be successful, we'll probably need your help.'

"I guess I was in such a state of shock that I found I could only pick at this wonderful lunch, and soon Marco announced it was time to go.

"This time, the limo took us to a private airfield where there was a small plane waiting to take us back to San Vida. As soon as we were in our seats, we took off and head back east, then dipped south in a big semi-circle. Our pilot explained that this *buttonhook* flight path would get us around the storm that was rapidly moving up the Gulf Stream.

"As a result our fight going back took twice as long, which I didn't like at all, but at least Marco filled in a bit of the time by giving us a few more details."

"We caught a break. Raymundo has decided to play poker tonight,' Marco explained. 'My guy says he has been bouncing off the walls and needed to get out of the compound. Poker and coke do it for him every time. The good news is that Joanie is alone in the house with only the nanny and one bodyguard. The bad news is that the one guy that's left is a real hard ass. But we've brought plenty of cash, so we're thinking he'll listen to reason. And if the past is any indication, Raymundo will be playing poker for at least three or four hours. That should give us enough time to get in and get out, and Maria will have her daughter again.'

"Once we landed in San Vida, there was a car waiting for us. At touchdown, Marco made a call. 'No shit,' he said and then listened for a few more seconds. 'Where are they now? Got it.'

"He leaned toward the driver and gave him some directions that didn't mean anything to me.

"'Somebody's following Raymundo's car,' Marco said. 'It's that old guy who hangs out with your husband.'

"'Sy?' I said. 'Is that his name?' Marco asked. 'I had my guy following Raymundo, and then he saw that Sy was on him, too. That's crazy, huh? It's turning into a parade. And we're about to join it.' The phone rang again. Once more, Marco listened and then whistled low. 'You gotta be kidding. We're almost there. Stay with the car.'

"'That Sy guy crashed into Raymundo's car and shot Raymundo's driver. I don't know why. But now he's got Raymundo in his car. Looks like they're heading toward the docks. I don't know what the hell is going on. said Marco.'

"We then drove to a row of broken-down warehouses, where we saw Sy's car parked in front of a building. Marco told his driver to park way down one of the rows of buildings so we could watch the door, but would be far enough away that we wouldn't be noticed. About ten minutes later, Marco's friend pulled up, ran over and jumped in our car. Just as he did so, we could see your car arrive.

We sat there with the rain now pounding on our car, steam on the windows, nobody saying anything…. It was unreal… eerie, all made worse by not knowing what was going on. I really thought I would scream. Then Marco said something to his guy in Spanish and it looked like they were just about to get out of our car when you came out of the building, got in yours and left. I didn't know whether to be more terrified or relieved that at least you were away from something bad."

"Marco said, 'Everything's getting more complicated. I don't know what the hell is happening inside, but we'll wait here till my guy takes a look.'

Chapter Twenty-Nine

It ain't what you know that gets you in trouble. It's what you know for sure that just ain't so that can wipe you out, or worse.
—Mark Twain

Sy and Norm arrived at our door just as Debbie was finishing her story. Sy had dropped Ozzie off at his own car. His work for the night was done.

They both embraced Debbie—even Sy, who definitely wasn't big on hugging. I quickly filled them in on what Debbie had told me.

Then it was my turn to provide the other less savory details. I described to Debbie how Sy had been trying to get a confession out of Raymundo, but was interrupted when he got a call from Ozzie saying he had located Waiterman and that he thought Waiterman might be able to lead us to Marilyn and Rylee. I then told her how Sy had left me with Raymundo, and how my first reaction was that I wanted to shoot him for what I believed he had done to us. But when I saw what Sy had put him through with the orange juice squeezer, I had second thoughts. "And I became even less sure about Raymundo's involvement, because of the way he kept insisting that he hadn't had anything to do with any kidnapping. Not Rylee. Not Marilyn. Not you and Maria, which I was just starting to consider blaming him for. It wasn't just what he said, but it was the way he said it. He is a

235

very tough guy and I'll bet he can stand a lot of pain. But if you heard and saw what I saw, you'd probably believe him too. So even as white hot angry as I had been, I had to conclude that he might be telling the truth. But I couldn't just let him go until I knew for sure. It also flashed through my mind about what the hell we were going to do with him if he wasn't involved. He was going to be one cranky son of a bitch when we untied him.

"I didn't get too hung up on that, because it wasn't too long after Sy left that he called me and told me what Waiterman had said about the old church. I told Sy that Raymundo was still tied up and wasn't going anywhere. Then I took off to meet the guys at the church."

"So, Debbie, you were with Marco the whole time?" Sy interjected.

Debbie nodded and continued her story. "As soon as Chance drove away from the building, Marco and his friend nodded to each other, and Marco said, 'We'll be right back.' The driver drove us up closer to the door, the guys jumped out, walked to the warehouse and went inside.

"Maria and I just looked at each other, bewildered. The windows were up in our car, and with the AC going, it was difficult to hear anything, but I thought I heard something that sounded like a champagne cork popping. In the next minute, Marco and his friend walked calmly out of the warehouse and got in our car. We backed down the row of buildings, Marco's friend got out, climbed in his car and followed us.

"Maria asked, 'Marco, what happened?'

"'I'll tell you all about it later, baby,' Marco said. 'Right now, let's go get your little girl.'

"From that point on, it seemed like everything was in slow motion. It took about twenty minutes, maybe more, to get to Maria's house. We were being followed by Marco's friend, and every once in a while, Marco's driver had to pull over to let him catch up. By now the water was flowing in the streets so bad I was concerned that we might be swept into the ditch or worse.

"When we got to the gate, Marco started to punch in the access code, but Maria said ruefully, 'He changed it after...I was about to say, "After you died."' She gave him the new one as he punched it in.

"We drove to the front of the house, got out, and approached the front door, while Marco's friend disappeared around to the back. Maria used her key to get us into the house. The bodyguard must have been watching the monitor, because as soon as we walked in, he appeared holding the biggest pistol I've ever seen. We could see he was conflicted. He seemed very unsure about what to do. Here he had Marco, who used to be his compatriot. And he also had the lady of the house, obviously on a mission to get her little girl. Talk about being stuck between a rock and a hard place.

"'Marco,' he said, 'I don't know what to say because we've got a problem here. Raymundo is out, and I can't let you take the little girl till he gets back.'

"Marco smiled at him. 'Raymundo won't be coming back.'

"The bodyguard heard the veiled remark and seemed to instinctively raise his gun. In that instant, his face exploded into a mass of red. He dropped like a sack of potatoes. Marco's friend was standing behind him, his own pistol still outstretched. Marco nodded at him and then turned to Maria.

"'I'm sorry you had to see that. But go get Joanie,' he said. 'Only pack what's absolutely necessary. We can buy clothes and stuff stateside.'

"The nanny, a Balboan woman in her late forties, was standing at the top of the stairs, frozen. Horrified, she had her hand over her mouth, not moving. She looked like a statue.

"'Annie,' Maria said in a calm voice, 'don't be afraid. Come help me get Joanie ready to go.' The woman was frozen to the spot, but Maria put a hand on her arm, and eventually she followed her to Joanie's room.

"Marco called after them, 'Go out the patio door. Don't bring Joanie through here.'

"I gagged. I almost threw up. I'd never seen anyone die before. It was horrible. I was afraid I was going to faint. Marco led me into the living room and sat me down on the couch. He walked over to the bar and poured some kind of liqueur into a glass. I wanted it to calm my nerves but remembered our baby just as I started to take a gulp. I spit it back in the glass just as we heard their footsteps on the patio. We walked past the dead body, trying not to look, and met Maria, Joanie, and Annie near the back door. Marco had a large wad of bills that he handed to Annie. Maria embraced her and said, 'Thank you for everything.'

"Annie held out her arms, hugged Maria, and said, 'Good luck. You've always been kind to me. You deserve happiness, miss.'

"It was another thirty-minute drive to get me home, but Marco did just as he said he would. His driver pulled up out front, and I hugged Maria and wished her a very, very good life. Then I got out, and they drove away. But almost immediately they stopped and backed up. Marco rolled down the window and said 'Don't forget your phone' as he handed it to me."

Chapter Thirty

What goes around, comes around.
—Well-worn Jewish expression

We sat speechless for a few moments. Finally, Sy spoke. "Well," he said, "that explains that."

"What?" Debbie said.

"We found Raymundo with a bullet in his brain."

Debbie gasped.

Sy almost smiled. "At first, I thought Chance had done it. But then I figured, nah, too much of a pussy."

The guys shared a glance at one another and kind of nodded in agreement and almost laughed. Marilyn and Debbie didn't think it was funny.

"But we still have to figure out what to do about this other thing," Norm said.

"What other thing?" asked Debbie.

Nobody wanted to say it.

I said, "Go ahead. Debbie needs to hear it all."

Sy said, "OK Debbie, here we go, but guaranteed you're not going to like it. All along we figured Raymundo had kidnapped Marilyn and Rylee. But it wasn't him. It was Johnny A."

Debbie gasped and slumped back on the sofa. "Johnny? He wouldn't. You've been friends since you were kids."

I said to her, "Not always. You remember a long time back I told you how I caught him cheating and had to fire him?"

Debbie said, "Yeah. But he can't still be holding a grudge about that. I mean you rehired him, right?"

"Well, there was a little more to it than just that. I had to… aw…hell, I broke his thumbs."

"Chance!"

"He was cheating a bunch of guys, including Mickey Spinello. If I hadn't handled it right, they would have killed him. They might have killed me too. It had to be done. There was no choice, but I guess Johnny never saw it that way. I shouldn't be too surprised."

I turned to Sy and Norm and said, "We need to meet Johnny tomorrow. Can't do it now. Too late. In the meantime, nobody say nothing to nobody."

"Should we meet in the Garden?" Norm asked.

"No," I said. "That will put his radar antenna up for sure. At this point, he doesn't know we've got the girls back or even about the Raymundo episode. So you should call him at eight in the morning and tell him nothing, other than that we're getting together at nine here at our place. That won't give him enough time to go do anything other than get here. Tell him that we're going to consider our options and that we are thinking about bringing the cops in. Say and do whatever you have to, to get him here. Just don't spook him.

"I don't think anybody has a clue about what's been going on, and we know he won't have time to get out to the church, so he won't suspect anything. We just have to ensure that Rylee and Marilyn are kept under wraps so that he doesn't see them. And, Sy, would you please get in touch with Ozzie? Let him know what's going on and have him come here in the morning, as well."

After Sy and Norm left, and Debbie and Marilyn had gone to bed, I just sagged into my chair. I was weak with exhaustion, but my mind was spinning. I poured myself a stiff drink and thought about the last twenty-four hours. I thought about my fear over losing Debbie. I thought about my terror that I might have lost my child. And I thought about Johnny and all the things we had done together. But mostly, I thought about killing him.

Chapter Thirty-One

In the casino industry the vig is the casino's revenue, often described as the house edge. It's the money the casino wins or extracts from the players. In the game of life.
Wives and girls friends are the vig.
—Seymour Harris, Rancho Mirage, California

Norm was the first to arrive, about eight thirty in the morning. He had nothing but bad news. He hadn't been able to reach Johnny. Five minutes later, Sy arrived. More bad news. Ozzie was worried that he had let the cat out of the bag. Apparently, after Sy dropped him off the previous night, he went to his girlfriend's apartment. Naturally, when he arrived looking like a drowned puppy, she wondered what happened to him, and he told her about the rescue. "And you'll never guess who she works for," Sy groaned. "She works in the office of the *San Vida Tribune*. What are the odds of that? And to make matters worse, she's an aspiring reporter. So after Ozzie went to sleep, she wrote up the story and called her editor with the scoop, obviously hoping it might get her a promotion. In the process, she also made a bunch of other calls. Ozzie's afraid by now Johnny will know what's up."

"Jesus Christ!" I exploded. "How could this happen? All people had to do was to keep their damn mouths shut. Now what? What the hell do we do now?"

It took a second or two for everyone to grasp the significance of what had gone down. Finally, Norm said, "Well, the first thing I should do is go to Johnny's apartment. It's a slim chance he'll still be there, but we should at least check it out."

"Yeah," Sy agreed. "We should check it out, but my bet is that he's long gone. He'll be off the island and on his way to who knows where."

"What about covering the marinas and the airport? Maybe he's not gone yet." I ventured. "Can we at least get some guys to check those out? Maybe someone saw something."

"What about bringing Greg in on this now?" suggested Norm.

"I still don't like getting the cops involved. We still have some dirty laundry that we need to clean up," said Sy emphatically.

Dumbfounded by this unexpected turn of events, everybody just kind of milled around the kitchen, having a coffee, talking, and not knowing what, if anything, should be done.

Still absolutely livid but calming down a bit, I finally said, "Well, there's no point just standing around here. I think Norm's right. Norm, you go to Johnny's place to see what you can find out. Sy, keep trying to contact Ozzie. When you do, ask him to go out to the marina at West End and to check that out. Sy, you can also check out the marinas here. I'll go to the airport, although I don't know what the hell I expect to find there. I don't think they'll give me any passenger lists, but at least I can ask around."

Everybody agreed and started to walk to the front door, when suddenly the doorbell rang.

Norm was the first to get there, and as he opened the door, in walked Ozzie with his customary greeting: "Hi guys. What's up?"

"What's *up?* Jesus, Ozzie. You know what's up. I thought we all agreed we were going to keep quiet about everything. And you've got to go and open up to your girlfriend?" I ranted.

"Easy, Chance," said Norm. "How could Ozzie know his gal was going to open her mouth? It was just a fluke."

"I know, boss. It be on me. No excuse. She's a little fox. Last night after a shower and a little poontang, we got to talkin', and she just got it out of me. I'm bein' honest now, I was feelin' pretty proud about us finding de girls an dat, plus I let my little head do my tinking instead of my big head…so I messed up."

"OK," I said, cooling down more. "We're just about to head out…"

"OK, boss, I got it. But I need to show you sometin' furst."

"What's that?"

"Best show you in de garage. Don't want no eyes on dis. Got to pull my car in. An best da ladies don' see."

Marilyn and Debbie had been standing there just listening to the guys. Debbie started to protest, but I was firm. "Please, gals, give us the kitchen. I don't know what Ozzie's going to show us, but until I see it, I don't know if you'd want to see it anyway."

The guys gathered in the garage as Ozzie backed in. I shut the garage door, and Ozzie popped the trunk.

The trunk lid flew up, and there was Johnny, arms and legs tied, with a cloth jammed in his mouth. Alive but with eyes as big as poker chips.

"Jesus, Ozzie. How? Where? How'd you find him?" All the guys spoke almost as one, trying to process what they were seeing.

With a lot more force than was necessary, Ozzie slammed the trunk shut as he said, "When me and my foxy chick get up dis mornin' about six turty, da first ting she do was tell me what she had done. She say this story goin' get her a job as reporta.

Man, I was a some pissed mutha! She know it, too. She get to cryin' first, den we get busy.

"Me an' her get on da jungle drums big-time. We phone everybody we know to watch fo' white dude tryin' to get off da island. Sy, you remember Flyboy? He de airplane mechanic for da private planes. He be my cell roomie fo' year when we in Dog Hill prison. We tight. He call back in 'bout an hour. Say he got eyes on da white motha. Dude about to get in a little prop plane. I tol' him don't let him go. I be dere in fifteen minutes. Flyboy went to pilot an' tol' him compression low on dat engine an' dat he should take udder plane. No problem. No biggie. By the time dey get out de udder plane from da hanger, I be dere. Just took a second. Me an' Flyboy scoop white dude, throw him in trunk. An' here we be."

Talk about a surprise. We were incredulous. Finally someone said, "All good, but what now?"

"Take him to the Garden," I said.

The Garden is at the rear of the casino in a separate building. Its door is just forty feet from the rear parking area that is used mostly for service and delivery vehicles. Ozzie and Sy drove over together, and after making sure nobody was watching, they backed their car in, parked, and hauled Johnny out of the trunk, unseen, and into the Garden. Norm and I had arrived just a few minutes before the three of them. For a few moments we just sat there trying to make sense of it all, and I knew I had to compose myself. I was so enraged I thought I might take one look at Johnny and try to strangle him with my bare hands. But I didn't want to do something stupid. When leaving the house I had even considered not taking my pistol. But I did. I had stuck the .38 in my belt, just at the small of my back and under my blazer.

We were watching for them, and as soon as they started up the walkway, Norm pushed open the door, and they shoved a terrified Johnny into the room. The door clicked shut. It felt like a tomb.

The guys had untied Johnny's legs, and now they untied his arms and took the cloth out of his mouth. We didn't have to worry about noise. The Garden was designed for situations like this. Soundproof. They pushed him onto the couch.

I pulled a chair over so I could sit opposite him. Johnny sat there stunned. Memories must have flooded back, a déjà vu moment.

I was seething, and with my face a foot from his, I demanded "I've only got one question for you—*why* did you kidnap my daughter and her grandmother?"

Johnny grimaced, and then the son of a bitch almost grinned. "Are you serious? I didn't kidnap nobody."

I stood up. I'd often heard the phrase "seeing red," but this was the first time I had experienced it for myself.

"My DAUGHTER!" I shouted at the top of my lungs. I pulled the pistol from my belt and rammed it into his forehead.

The defiance in his eyes melted away and was replaced by raw fear. "I swear…"

Through gritted teeth, I said, "You held a grudge against me all this time. But you're too much of a coward to deal with me. No, you had to kidnap a little girl and an old woman. And then you killed them!"

Johnny's eyes doubled in size. "No, no, no," he said. "Chance, I didn't kill nobody. I swear."

"You kidnapped them, and you killed them," I said, trying a con.

"Chance," Johnny was near tears. "Chance, on my mother's grave, I never killed them. When they were left at the church, they were OK. Both of them were just fine! They were safe!"

Sy, Norm, and I looked at one another. Maybe this confession wouldn't hold up in court, but it worked for us.

Johnny was sobbing now. "I swear, Chance…I swear…"

I pulled back the hammer on the .38.

I felt the raw power of this life-and-death moment. I could barely get the words out. "Why wait? I should finish this here and now."

Johnny sank off the couch and onto his knees.

Sy stepped forward, the one guy who hated Johnny maybe even more than me. He put his hand on the barrel of the .38 and gently pushed it aside.

"You don't want to do this, Chance," he stated solemnly.

"Sy, I've never wanted anything more in my entire life."

Sy shook his head. "You're not a killer, pal. Right now all you want is for this piece of garbage to be dead. But a week from now, or a year from now, it'll come back at you. It don't bother some people. Some people even like it. But you ain't one of them. You have a heart. You have a conscience. It might feel good in this second, but it'll eat at you for the rest of your life. I know you, and I know it would chew at you forever."

Norm nodded. "Sy's right, Chance. Let it go."

"I can't let him go."

"I said let *it* go, not let *him* go," Norm corrected.

Sy and Ozzie grabbed Johnny by his arms and lifted him to his feet. "I'll take care of him," Sy said. Johnny looked around with terrified eyes and tried to pull himself from Sy's grasp, but for somebody who looked like a grandfather, the man had a grip like a vice.

I turned and looked at Sy. "What are you doing? You won't let me shoot him, but you're going to kill him yourself?"

"No, I'm not going to shoot him. My gun is just to keep him focused." Turning to Johnny Sy snarled, "you lucky bastard. The girls aren't dead. Wet, terrified, but not dead, no thanks to you. They could have drowned lying on the floor of that church. But they're going to be Ok, and now we're going to walk you to Ozzie's car and you're going to be outta here. We're going to ship you off the island, and we never want to see you again. You got that? If we ever see, or even hear from you again, you'll *wish* you were dead."

Then Sy twisted Johnny's arms behind his back and again slipped the plastic handcuffs over his wrists. Visibly relieved, all Johnny could do was nod.

Sy then reached for the Kleenex box on the table stand, grabbed some, and jammed a wad into Johnny's mouth as they headed to the door. "Take one last look at him. Johnny's going on a short trip. We'll take him across the Gulf Stream and leave him in Florida with only the clothes on his back. And if he has any brains at all, he'll be out of our lives forever."

I stood there for a moment, again just relishing the thought of killing him on the spot. I hated him with every fiber of my being. But finally I turned, put the gun back into my belt, clicked open the dead bolt lock, and let them out of the room and out of my life.

Chapter Thirty-Two

For me to have any more luck, I'd have to be twins.
—Don Wilson, Okotoks, Alberta, 2009

Three months later, Debbie presented me with a beautiful baby: Daniel Adam Daly, seven pounds, fifteen ounces. It was a dream come true. Marilyn was over the moon at having a second grandchild, and Rylee seemed to think we had presented her with a special kind of living doll just for her. Which, I suppose we did. She was proud and delighted to be a big sister. I figured that would change when they were teenagers, but, thankfully, we still had a few years before that.

As for me, I'm happy. Life's good. Rylee's eleven. Danny is seven. They're both smart, good-looking kids. Rylee is turning into her mom, whom I treasure and love dearly. Business is good. The Diamond Resorts' Board of Directors gave me the time I needed to demonstrate how profitable the casinos could be, and within nine months the performance charts showed the trajectory of a hockey stick. With those results, it wasn't a difficult decision for the Board to reject the overtures from the drug cartel. We have fourteen casino operations in the network now, all just humming along.

Sy's gone now. Several years ago, Ozzie found him slumped over at the kitchen table in his condo. He died having his morning coffee. I've always thought it was a rather inglorious way for a professional killer to end up. But I'm glad he found peace. He may not have been the most important person in my life, but he sure was near the top. His wise council probably kept me from making a horrible mistake that last day with Johnny. And he was right. Even though I was filled with rage toward the maggot who kidnapped my little girl, I'm not a killer. If I had killed Johnny, I probably would never have been able to live with myself.

As it is, I never heard about or saw Johnny again. From time to time I would ask Sy what happened to him, but he'd never let on. In fact, he only acknowledged Johnny's existence twice and both times he'd been drinking. Once, he said that he had changed his mind about what to do with Johnny. Whatever the hell that meant. And another time, when I asked where he dropped Johnny off, he just looked at me, smiled and said, "Oh, you mean Alpo." Sy didn't smile often. It took me a long time to figure that one out, but when I did, I shuddered.

I never think of Johnny anymore. Except when somebody brings up his name, or from time to time when I hear the wild dogs howl.

Acknowledgments

I'm a little further down the road since my last book, *It's Always a Game*.

It was with considerable reluctance that I took on this project. But surprisingly so many people had graciously asked what happened to Chance after the ending of the last book, that I eventually got up enough steam to write this sequel.

My thanks to my family, friends, including those who buoyed my flagging energy with their constant harassment, asking "when is your book going to be done?" Also thanks to those who were so helpful in the editing process, the idea department, and the information department, including Jon Wood, Lloyd Shinn, Linda Wilson, Doug Tannas, Shannon Tannas, Laverne McGonigal, Spencer Mohler, Ronda Beatty (a great editor), Ryan Ziegler, Jim Beatty, Bill Goldberg, Bruce Klippenstein, Dan Beatty, Heather Green, Patsy Stang, Rick Sanderson, Chuck Connolly, Debbie Sanderson, Frank Thompson, Brent Hooey, Jerry Stevenson, "Murph," and Robert Osborne, a true hero whose character appears in this book. Whether it was helping to edit, or if I needed information, or inspiration, or sometimes just when I was stuck on where to go with the story, each of those above came to my rescue, and I'm grateful.

And, of course, thanks to my family for making my life so wonderful.

I am grateful to my sons, Dan Beatty and Adam Dingwell, and my son-in-law, Jason McGonigal. The three of you amaze me with your exploits and business acumen. And to my grandchildren Sean, Declan, Megan, Kaleb, Emma, Rylee, Quinn, Addy and my buddy Gabriel Bechard. And my thanks to the best daughters-in-law in the world: Debbie Beatty, Jaime West, Christina McGonigal and Amanda Dingwell.

And, finally, my thanks to Wendy Dingwell, and Laverne McGonigal. You gals spent a considerable portion of your lives trying to keep me between the ditches. In the process you made me a better person and my world a better place.

Gracias,

Douglas Beatty

The Author

J W Douglas Beatty was born in Toronto, Canada and raised by parents whose lifestyle included Wednesday and Sunday night poker games, and who would bet on whether or not the sun would come up the next day, as long as he got the right odds. He was playing cards at five and going to Craps games with his dad at fifteen. At Etobicoke High School he operated the lunch hour Craps game and the Three Star Hockey Pool. He ran card games and had a small bookmaking operation in his teens and into his twenties. During this period, Beatty also probably spent far too much time playing poker, Hearts, Gin, pool, checkers, chess, golf, and any other gambling game that had live cash action.

Leaving school at fifteen he followed a gambling path but also found time to play hockey in the Toronto Marlborough's Hockey chain and coached a number of kid's hockey teams and Little League baseball teams.

Married at eighteen and with a child at twenty, Beatty moved to Las Vegas, becoming a Craps dealer at the Fremont Hotel. Returning to Canada with considerable gaming experience, and having studied the detection and prevention of illegal gambling techniques, he had occasion to work with the police departments in both Ontario and Manitoba. In both provinces, he helped to bring about the arrest and conviction of a number of card and dice cheats. During his somewhat varied career, Beatty lived in West Toronto and Toronto Island; Freeport, Bahamas, where he was on the Board of Directors of the YMCA and was the President of the Canadian Men's Club of the Bahamas. Beatty was also the founder and Commissioner of the Bahamian Baseball Little

League which is still in existence today. He also lived in Las Vegas, Nevada; Denton, Texas; Winnipeg, Manitoba; Calgary; Red Deer; and, presently Okotoks, Alberta in the summer, and Rancho Mirage, California, in the winter.

From the Author

In recent years my gambling has been confined to owning many (mostly slow) racehorses, the occasional poker game, and probably too much golf. A few years ago I won $1,500 in a golf proposition bet by playing eighteen holes right-handed, eighteen holes left-handed, and eighteen holes backward, all in the same day. Gabe Kaplan of *Welcome Back, Kotter* fame knocked me out of a celebrity poker tournament a bunch of years ago, and I've had to accept that my poker playing has not improved since.

A few years ago, we shot a television pilot for my first book, *It's Always a Game,* in Toronto. It remains to be seen whether it will get any traction, but it did help me to know once and for all that I have absolutely no desire to be an actor.

Looking back, I realize that I've lived a number of very different lives—some interesting, some dangerous, some successful, and some pretty sketchy. And as my brother says, probably one of my greatest accomplishments is that I've lived to tell about them.

But stay tuned, I can hardly wait to see what I'm going to do next.

BTW to help pay off my gambling debts, (current and future…), paperback or ebook versions of my books can be obtained from Amazon.ca or by sending your check to the writer. I have a zillion copies in my garage.

Enjoy!

J W Douglas Beatty
doug@douglasbeatty.com

More books by Douglas Beatty

amazon.com

www.ingramcontent.com/pod-product-compliance
Lightning Source LLC
Chambersburg PA
CBHW051542260626
47170CB00003B/1065